ALI A. MAZRUI

The Trial of Christopher Okigbo

HEINEMANN
London Ibadan Nairobi

Heinemann Educational Books Ltd
48 Charles Street London WIX 8AH
PMB 5205 Ibadan – POB 25080 Nairobi
EDINBURGH MELBOURNE TORONTO AUCKLAND
HONG KONG SINGAPORE KUALA LUMPUR NEW DELHI

ISBN 0 435 90097 8

Printed in England by Fletcher & Son Ltd.
Norwich

In January, 1968, a tall young man, who was a famous television personality, returning to Nairobi from a visit to his family in Mombasa, was killed by his own car somewhere beyond Voi. In October, 1967, a lean young poet, in the uniform of a major, was killed by his own country on the war front at Nsukka.

This novel of ideas is dedicated to 'Giraffe' and to Chris Okigbo – In Memoriam.

PREFACE TO SECOND IMPRESSION

I believe it was the evening of May 30th, 1967. My wife and I had just sat down for dinner in our house on Kasubi View in Kampala – named after the view it afforded of the tombs of the Baganda Kings. I had my transistor radio on the dining table for the eight o'clock news. The first item was that Colonel Ojukwu, the Ibo military leader, had declared the Eastern Region of Nigeria an independent republic, the Republic of Biafra.

This was the act of secession – the civil war had yet to start. But my imagination had already taken the leap. In one staggering flash I saw many of the faces of Nigerians I had known as a student in my younger days; I saw them with guns, and I saw the guns aiming at each other. It is curious how an item on a news bulletin can quickly crystallize into an image steeped in personal memories. To my surprise my eyes filled up, I breathed in sharply, and broke down and wept. Molly, astonished by my reaction to the news item, rose from her chair in startled bewilderment.

Then there was that other dinner some months later. This was in Mombasa in the Old Town. It was dinner at the home of Kim, a very old friend of mine. Among the guests was Mohamed Salim Said, better known among his friends as *Giraffe*. This was because of his height – he was exceptionally tall by local standards, though I do not remember how many inches above six feet Mohamed was. I had known Mohamed Giraffe even longer than I had known Kim. Giraffe had been a childhood friend of mine; we had played together, attended mosque together, and had fist fights on occasion. In our younger days as children I was the bully, though Giraffe was somewhat bigger in size. But as we were having dinner in Mombasa on the very last day of 1967 he towered above me so convincingly that I would not have dreamt of provoking him!

It was a cheerful dinner, that one – unlike that moment of weakness at Kasubi View some months previously, when Molly and I had been listening to the transistor radio. We discussed a number of subjects, Giraffe and I, in what turned out to be our last meal together.

I left the next day for Dar es Salaam to attend a conference. That was Monday. On Tuesday Giraffe left Mombasa to return to Nairobi. He had been in broadcasting and television for a number of years, either full-time or free lance.

I got the news when I was at the conference in Dar es Salaam. Giraffe was dead. It had been a road accident. He had left Mombasa in the evening with a friend, an Inspector of Police and one other passenger. Giraffe had been driving. He had seemed in an excessive hurry, and would not stop at Voi for a cup of tea, as his friend had suggested. Somewhere past Voi the car had a puncture. While the car was still in motion Giraffe did what turned out to be the most careless act of his life – he opened the door to see if the puncture was on his side of the car. The car was still moving fairly fast. The door was flung open more widely, and Giraffe was thrown out, plunging in a somersault into the darkness of the night. The car got out of control and turned over in a deadly somersault of its own. And then that bizarre act of impersonal vindictiveness, as it were – the car went crashing on to the head of its former driver, lying dazed on the ground, and then rested over his dead body. It seems virtually certain that Giraffe was killed not by his own somersault when he was thrown out of the car, but by the incredible coincidence that a car which had overturned after he was thrown out should have ended up cracking his skull.

The details of the story were provided by his passengers, the Inspector of Police and the wife of a friend. To the present day the woman has not fully recovered from that episode. As the survivors were struggling out of the car that fateful night, and were feeling under the car, she touched something cold, wet, and messy on the ground; she looked and saw that the substance was Giraffe's brain. For a long time afterwards she went cold with terror every time she associated her hand with that substance she had touched in the dark that night on the way to Nairobi.

The impact of Giraffe's death upon me turned out to be also

very deep, but for reasons which were far less obvious. It is true that Giraffe had been a boyhood friend of mine. And in my first years as a person living away from home, with a flat of my own at the Mombasa Institute of Muslim Education in the early 1950s, Giraffe and I shared that flat briefly. Then we knew each other in England – I as a University student, he as a broadcaster trainee at the B.B.C. in London. When we finally returned to East Africa, we kept in touch but not all that closely. He was then at Nairobi and heavily involved in broadcasting and television. He had a way of knowing whenever I would be in Nairobi. Sometimes he would even be at the airport waiting for me. Sometimes I would hear an announcement on the loudspeaker beckoning me to the telephone. I never fully discovered what his sources of information about my movements were – perhaps it was enough that he was interested and followed them. And yet in spite of this, ours was a friendship which did not entail regular communication with each other. We hardly ever wrote letters to each other. Most of the time when I was in Kampala and he was in Nairobi, we seldom thought of each other, but simply went about our daily business.

And yet when he was killed I felt an emptiness that I had never felt before – not even when I lost my father way back in 1947. Other friends of mine had died before, and I had grieved for them. When I was an undergraduate a Spanish friend of mine committed suicide only a few hours after I had seen him at the Students' Union. I was shocked, indeed shattered, for a day or two. But with Giraffe the anguish seemed to be going on day after day, week after week.

I discovered then that I was passing through a major emotional crisis involving two kinds of pain. One kind was directly personal, the sudden and violent death of a friend. But the other kind was public anguish personalized, and this was the painful drama of the Nigerian civil war. The personal anguish over Giraffe and the public anguish over the Nigerian civil war seemed to merge in ways which were quite incomprehensible to me, but which went a long way towards explaining the depression I was passing through.

Between my memorable supper at Kasubi View marking the tragic birth of Biafra, and my last dinner with Giraffe in Mombasa, Christopher Okigbo was killed. The Nigerian poet had decided that he was, first and foremost, an Ibo. He had put on his uniform to fight for Biafra, and he had died for Biafra.

Curiously enough Chris Okigbo became the point of contact between my personal anguish over Giraffe and my internalized public anguish over Nigeria. The death of Okigbo was a fusion of the personal and the social, the private and the public, the poetic and the political.

As Okigbo, Giraffe, and the civil war together held reins controlling my moods in early 1968, a thought occurred to me. Why not write a novel? Why not write a novel set in the Hereafter, with dead men living again, and live issues debated by the dead? Why not put Christopher Okigbo and Giraffe on a platform of destiny beyond the grave? In short, dear Ali Mazrui, why not fictionalize your anguish?

The human imagination is a strange stimulus. I started to write. If fictionalizing my anguish was therapeutic, it was also slow and tense. It is true that at some times I write more slowly than at others, but even in my slowest periods I am about average in speed. Yet those weeks early in 1968 were weeks of frustration. I wrote ten little chapters, and then gave up the whole enterprise. The attempt seemed to drain my energies : I gave up in exhaustion and despair.

On the Nigerian front my exhaustion may have been due to the nature of my predicament. My moral support was for the Federal side; my sympathies were with the Ibo. It was that kind of tragedy – a tragedy of rights in conflict. I loved the Ibo and hated Biafra. My position was publicly known at Makerere – but not the agony which went with such a position.

Months passed. The war in Nigeria continued. Giraffe's presence in my life continued. And then Molly thought of what we later light-heartedly described as 'the pilgrimage'. Why not drive along the road where Giraffe had met his death? If I could not fictionalize my anguish, could I at least trivialize it?

We took the train to Nairobi and then hired a car. It was December 1969, and December was the last full month of Giraffe's life. Molly drove, and we really became quite lighthearted about the memory of Giraffe. We even mused about the possibility of erecting a statue, more than life size, of the animal giraffe, with its long front legs and shorter hind legs, and that neck towering above the rest of the species. We laughed at our own jokes. It was a bid to trivialize a painful presence in our lives. Of course Molly knew Giraffe and liked him, but to her he was simply another friend of mine. However, my depression over Giraffe's death and the Nigerian civil war had now become part of her life. She had a mission to seek a way out for both of us. And so we joked as she drove me down the Mombasa road on our way to the sea.

Immediately on arrival in Mombasa we went to see my mother. There were the usual greetings. And what's more, there were the usual people around, some having come to visit my mother precisely because her son was about to arrive. We sat down and discovered that a conversation had been going on. Both the English and the Swahili word for 'giraffe' kept recurring. Molly and I looked at each other, curious and somewhat concerned. I asked what it was all about.

And then this new story unfolded itself. Basheikh, a Mombasa boy who had made good in the police and had become the third highest ranking official in the Kenya Police, had just been killed as he was driving down from Nairobi to Mombasa. How had he met his death? He was driving down to Mombasa with a friend, when all of a sudden a giraffe emerged from a bush. The giraffe was startled by the car, raised its massive forelegs in bewilderment, and then brought them down, crashing into the roof of the Volkswagen. The animal then, in freeing its legs once again, sent the car and its passengers rolling into the bush in one mighty kick of animal power.

The animal disappeared into the dark. The two passengers lay trapped in an overturned car in the bush. Mohamed felt a wet trickle, warm. No, it was not his own blood. It was Basheikh bleeding heavily. The roof, sunk massively in by the giraffe's feet, had both made deep wounds into Basheikh and broken his shoulder blade. Mohamed called out 'Basheikh'. Basheikh answered him once weakly; he then lost consciousness and bled to death.

A couple of days later Molly and I left Mombasa to return to Nairobi. Our pilgrimage in that bid to trivialize Giraffe's death had received a serious setback. Giraffe had been killed in the evening of the Muslim festival of Idd. Basheikh had been killed on Christmas eve. There had been a policeman in the car which was attacked by a giraffe in December 1969. There was a Mohammed involved in the accident of 1968 – Giraffe himself. There was a Mohammed in Basheikh's car – the fellow passenger who lived to tell the tale. But the most startling of all coincidences from the point of view of my pilgrimage lay in that simple story which the *East African Standard* reported on December 27th, 1969 – the story that a giraffe had suddenly emerged on to the high road, and occasioned one of the most unusual road accidents of all time.

As we were driving on, a car by the roadside came into view. It was a Volkswagen. A policeman was standing by its side, keeping guard. Yes, it was that car. The roof was smashed in, the windscreen shattered, and on the glass windows of the Volkswagen was a lot of dry blood. The policeman confirmed that this was the car in which Superintendent Basheikh had met his fate. It was discovered in the bush, with one dead man and one wounded and very weary passenger. It had been retrieved on to the roadside. It was shortly to be towed away from the scene of that bizarre accident.

Giraffe's presence in my life had, for the time being, refused to be exorcized. And the Nigerian civil war still raged. Molly and I staggered back home – a mission unfulfilled.

January was the month which followed. January was the month in which Giraffe was killed. January saw at last the end of the Nigerian civil war. One important dimension in the complex psychological picture of my depression had been eased by the end of the war. Not long afterwards I was on a plane from Rome to Tokyo. It was a long flight, and my mind returned once again to that first endeavour to deal with my state. I had begun by wanting to fictionalize it, and had given up the attempt after ten short halting chapters. And then I had attempted a second strategy – the strategy to trivialize. Destiny had conspired to enact a tragedy of coincidences affecting a Volkswagen on the Mombasa road. Should I now return to fiction for therapy?

On that flight from Rome to Tokyo the remainder of my novel, *The Trial of Christopher Okigbo*, was conceived in outline. I knew that on my return to Kampala I would have only about two weeks before having to travel again – this time to Cairo to give a series of lectures. I resolved on that trip to Tokyo that in those two weeks I would attempt to complete *The Trial*.

I did just that. I completed the book at a pace of writing staggeringly different from the pace at its beginning. I later mused about this phenomenon and how much it told us about the relationship between emotional involvement and ease of communication. The first part of my novel, the part which was written in 1968, is stylistically different from the rest. When I wrote the second part Michael Okenimpke, at the time a graduate student at Makerere, had served as my Ibo consultant. When the novel was completed, I gave it to him for comment and suggestions. He noticed that the novel was a little slow in taking off, but he was of the opinion that the slowness was artistically defensible in view of the intensity of the middle part of the novel – the trial itself. What Michael did not know at the time was that the first part had been written two years before the more intense portions.

My secretary at the time, Anna Gourlay, was even more critical of the first few chapters – arguing that too much patience was demanded of the reader.

The publisher, Heinemann in London, sent the novel to Chinua Achebe, their editorial advisor and someone who was himself deeply involved on the side of Biafra during the war. Achebe also commented on the slowness of the first few chapters. Again Achebe did not know the circumstances in which those chapters had been written.

By a curious paradox we might therefore say that the chapters which were written at a time of intense emotional upset turned out to be less gripping and more indifferent in tone than the chapters which were written two years later, when my depression was waning. In other words, the greater the emotional involvement of the writer, the lesser is his capacity to emotionally involve the reader. In some sense the first few chapters were a spontaneous, if halting overflow of powerful emotions, to use Wordsworth's formula. And yet a number of readers independently of each other saw that part of the novel in terms of its incapacity to involve the reader adequately. But after the Nigerian civil war my emotional state became more controlled.

And I wrote the remainder of the book furiously, within two weeks. The judgement of those who read the manuscript was that these hurriedly written parts, produced in a period of less emotional strain, had paradoxically turned out to be more gripping.

In the novel I put Okigbo, a Nigerian poet, on trial on two charges. The first charge was the more obvious political one – that he had subordinated the ideal of Nigeria to the vision of Biafra. The second charge was the Okigbo had decided that he was an Ibo first and an artist second. Counsel for Salvation in the trial is Hamisi – a tall man from Mombasa, who had been killed on his way to Nairobi, and who had once in the Herebefore discussed Okigbo's poetry on the B.B.C. African Service.

This novel has a dedication. Let me conclude with that dedication as it appears following the title page:

"In January, 1968, a tall young man who was a famous television personality, returning to Nairobi from a visit to his family in Mombasa, was killed by his own car somewhere beyond Voi. In October, 1967, a lean young poet, in the uniform of a major, was killed by his own country on the warfront at Nsukka.

This novel of ideas is dedicated to Giraffe and to Chris Okigbo – In Memoriam."

Kampala, Uganda.   *A.A.M.*

1

Hamisi dragged himself up from the ground. He was still a little dazed by it all. The railway track was still there but that one-eyed monster that had suddenly emerged upon him from nowhere had as readily dissolved into nowhere. The trees around looked different, more shadowy, but acquiring with that shadow a sense of deep and timeless presence. The buildings around had also undergone a mystifying transformation. There was a stamp of modernity about them that was somehow combined with a sense of infinite age. To him, whose memories were of a different world, the whole atmosphere around was an agony of incongruity. Newness and a sense of the ancient combined in the personality of every item within vision. And even the intricate network of a cobweb that had spread itself out between two branches exuded the power of clinical modernity. That there were clouds in the sky he soon noticed, but again their relationship to his place in the universe seemed to have tilted a little. The clouds had a greater immediacy without necessarily being any nearer to him. It was as if a great artist had shifted the cloud-world just slightly in its position to give a greater perspective of integration with the trees and structures below. Indeed, the clouds and the cobweb between those two branches were more clearly part of the same universe than they ever were in the world which Hamisi could now only vaguely remember.

As he was standing there trying to comprehend the nature of his environment he suddenly heard a voice saying, 'Oh, there you are, Hamisi.'

He turned round. He saw a man and a woman, neither of whom looked in the least familiar. In fact, they too, though clearly fellow Africans, had this dual personality of newness and timeless ancestry. But they were not old. On the contrary, they both seemed to be in either their late twenties or early thirties, but for a moment, it occurred to Hamisi that they must have been the same age for at least a thousand years. The man was wearing a *kanzu*, beautifully embroidered with silk around the neck and from the central point at the front of the neck all the way down to the hem of the garment. The woman's dress reminded Hamisi a little of Punjabi dress – a blouse that came down nearly to the knees with smart pajama-like pants touching the ghostly grass below. They both wore smiles which, had it not been for the chilling momentary incongruity of the whole environment, would have suitably been described as warm.

The man extended his hand to Hamisi and said, 'My name is Abiranja. We have been expecting you.'

Hamisi shook hands with him and then turned to accept the hand of the girl. Hamisi was expecting Abiranja to say either, 'and this is my wife,' or 'my girl-friend'. Instead, Abiranja said, 'This is Salisha, my companion.'

Hamisi thought, 'Companion, though usually applicable to both wives and girl-friends, is a rather strange usage in this context.'

Hamisi was still speculating about this usage when Abiranja's voice brought him back to the greater mysteries of his situation. 'You must still be wondering what it is all about – why this place looks so unfamiliar to you, how you came to be here and why the whole atmosphere wears a veil of strange timelessness. But in fact the explanation is quite simple, though I suggest you wait until we get home before you try to understand anything. For the time being a mood of mental resignation might well be the healthiest to adopt. Give up the attempt to reason it out.'

Hamisi willingly drifted into acceptance of that advice. He gave up the weary task of trying to understand.

A short while later they were sitting in Abiranja's home. The items of furniture and decoration were not unusual in themselves except for this feeling of persistent ambiguity about them. Apart from the three-piece suite, which was the most modern piece of furniture that Hamisi had ever seen, the room was dominated by a huge shield on the side wall. By way of explanation Abiranja said:

2

'You are wondering what the shield is. It is the one which Chaka, the Zulu conqueror, used in the battle of Umbutera.'

But the explanation of the shield's presence paled into insignificance as Hamisi contemplated the questions provoked by the shield's ancestry.

Salisha was about to serve some food when Hamisi ventured to ask if he could have a bath first before eating. Abiranja said, 'Yes, you are entitled to one bath as a new arrival. But you will have to go to a special place for that as it is an elaborate ritual. It is a more fundamental bath than you have ever had before. But after this first bath people here are entitled to swim any time they like, but not to have a bath as such. Swimming is an exercise and pleasure; but a bath is an exercise in cleansing. That is why we never have baths.'

Hamisi, again in a mood of despair, said he would settle at least for the use of a toilet before eating. Abiranja said, 'Oh that! I'd forgotten about it. Yes, of course you will continue to need toilet facilities until your body is fully acclimatised.'

Hamisi went to the toilet of Abiranja's home. Abiranja had to go and get him a special key for it, and it took his host at least ten minutes to find the key, as if they had had no occasion to need it for quite a while. They opened the lavatory. It was spotlessly clean; so clean that it could not have been used for quite a time. The evidence that it had not been used was not an accumulation of undisturbed dust, but simply a climate of clinical isolation from the rest of the life of the house. Hamisi used the lavatory and then returned to the sitting-room. Salisha then proceeded to serve food which was unfamiliar in visual character, but yet strangely attractive in taste. The drink she served reminded Hamisi of *sharubati*, a Swahili drink of Persian origin. But again, it wasn't quite that, though even the taste was reminiscent of *sharubati*. The meal was somewhat silent, partly because Hamisi had too many questions to ask and he decided not to start at all and partly because his host and hostess wanted to postpone all, demanding conversation until after Hamisi had had his initiation sleep.

The initiation sleep was simple. It was just slumber which

3

overcame him after his first meal in this strange land. He fell comfortably asleep sitting up in his chair as soon as he had finished eating.

2

Hamisi opened his eyes. He felt much less tense and uncertain than when he had first opened his eyes near the railway tracks some time before. The room was still Abiranja's. He now noticed something he had not observed before – bookshelves in the room. There was also a book on a table near the seat which had previously been occupied by Salisha. It was a thin book of poetry. He could not see the title properly from where he sat, but he could decipher the name of the poet. It was Christopher Okigbo. He looked at the rest of the room. There were other items of furnishing that he had not noticed before. Were they there before, he wondered? Before he could adequately grapple with this question, Salisha entered the room, saw him awake and called out to Abiranja.

'I hope you have had a good rest,' Salisha said, while they both waited for Abiranja. Hamisi said yes and was about to start asking questions when Abiranja came into the room. Abiranja recognized immediately the signs of critical curiosity in Hamisi's eyes; the moment was approaching when he would no longer be able to resist asking questions about the cumulative mysteries of his situation.

'I know, I know,' said Abiranja. 'You can no longer stand the burdens of ignorance. Very well, let us all sit together and see if we can at last help you to understand.'

Abiranja then asked Hamisi to try hard and recollect what was the last thing he had thought of before he woke up near the railway track. Hamisi tried hard for a while, but the mysteries of the last few hours had been too confusing to permit an easy flow of prior reminiscence. Why did he have only one more bath left for

4

the rest of his days? And what was this business about dispensing with the daily communion with nature in the lavatory? The cobweb between those branches, was it a case of ancient modernity, or modernized age? The clouds glimpsed in the perspective of integration with the cobweb between the branches. And why did that *sharubati* taste so different?

But his mind was drifting. He was seeking answers to the present instead of memories of the past. The only relevant question in the circumstances was for him to ask himself what he was doing by the railway tracks just before Abiranja and Salisha arrived. He tried hard. First, the agony was simply the agony of attempting to remember. But then Abiranja and Salisha noticed the look of perplexity in Hamisi's eyes change to one of intense concentration. Next came the pain of hard thinking; then a gradual dawn of fragmentary recollection, followed by a powerful, fearful scream. Abiranja and Salisha let Hamisi shake and groan for a while. Gradually, the torment subsided. Hamisi lifted his eyes and what remained now were the last stages of a battle between partial comprehension and the gradual accumulation of mysteries.

Hamisi started to relate what he could remember. He had left home in his car at the end of the first day of Idd. The day had been hectically joyous with the feasts of Mombasa to celebrate the annual pilgrimage to Mecca. The big fair for the children, with its swings, Indian snacks, gambling games, and less serious forms of make-believe; stalls selling *vitoria, mabungo*, mangoes and other African fruit had been in a full, flourishing life. But Hamisi was in a hurry to get back to Nairobi where he was starting a new job. He had decided to travel at night and had agreed to give a lift to his friend.

As they approached Voi, Ali reminded Hamisi about the idea of stopping for a cup of tea. But Hamisi seemed more impatient than ever – 'We must push on! Surely you are not thirsty yet. We can stop by the roadside later and have a drink. What would we do with our flask of tea if we stopped at Voi now and used the restaurant?'

Ali protested but Hamisi had a way of joking everything away in moments of tension. When he felt strongly enough about something Hamisi was inclined to impose his will on others but it had always been remarkable how very few people were ever offended by this. He managed by the warmth of his personality and evident desire to save the feelings of others to marry ambition to sociability. What might easily have become an aggressive personality with a strong will of its own was converted in him into a figure that commanded both respect and indulgence. Hamisi did not stop at Voi; the car moved on.

It was about seven miles from Voi when something started to go wrong with the car.

'It's a puncture,' said Ali.

Hamisi said, 'Yes, and I think it's on my side.'

That was when he made the most critical move of his life. With the car still in motion, Hamisi opened his door slightly to peep out. He wanted to see in that moonlight whether it was indeed the wheel on his side of the car which was punctured. There was a sharp shout from Ali – 'Watch out!' Hamisi turned to look. His car had already moved to the middle of the road and right in front of him was the huge light of a train. Allah – was it a train? As he tried to regain control of the car, his door was thrown completely open. The dazzling power of the train light seemed to be tilting – his own car was taking a sharp swerve. To his horror he suddenly found himself somersaulting in the air. There was a crash. He saw the moon falling. Or was it the big light of the train? God! It was both! The moon half covered by the shadow of the train engine, both falling towards him from the skies. He gave a shout and tried to roll away from them. But there seemed to be thousands of chains pinning him down where he was. He stretched out his arm to push back the moon and the massive engine falling upon him. There was a flash as if the moon had exploded into a thousand pieces. Then that ghastly pain on his head as total darkness engulfed him. But was it the moon? Was it a train? Or was it his own car?

As Hamisi was trying to remember all this in the company of Abiranja and Salisha the succession of events seemed to expand.

But in fact it had all been compressed within seconds from the time of the sight of the train approaching, the loss of control of the car, the spin in mid-air as he was thrown out of the door, the crash on to the ground, and the descending moon and engine destined for his head. Another groan convulsed him as he shook with the torment of remembered terror. Suddenly the whole universe was echoing with the words:

> *Watchman for the watchword*
> *at* Heavengate;
>
> *out of the depths my cry:*
> *give ear and hearken . . .*
>
> *The stars have departed,*
> *the sky in monocle*
> *surveys the worldunder.*
>
> *The stars have departed,*
> *and I – where am I?*

3

It was night-time, but the sitting-room had automatic lighting. Darkness enveloped only the outer world. Within the building, however, light persisted independently of what went on outside. There was a gadget in the room, but this was not to put on the light, only to control or modify it according to taste and requirements. It was like a little wheel half-protruding from the wall. If turned to the right it increased the intensity of lighting in the room; if turned to the left, it could reduce it down to utter darkness.

'Did the natural light in After-Africa come from the sun as it did in the Herebefore?' Hamisi wondered.

He leaned back in his chair. At the other end of the room was Salisha knitting a table-mat for the vase that Abiranja had newly acquired. It was from a collection given to Sundiata, Emperor of ancient Mali, as a gift from the Sultan of Marrakesh.

Abiranja himself was out for the evening on a mission with other friends. The thought of antiques from the Herebefore was evoking a new concentration in the mind of Hamisi. Chaka's mighty shield was looking down upon him from its wall behind Salisha's chair; Sundiata's vase was casually placed near a coffee-table as Salisha knitted away at the table-mat on which it was to rest. There was a certain ambivalence in the situation – a relic of the Herebefore dying and therefore surviving entire in the Here-after, and the quiet presence of Salisha in her late twenties, modest and self-effacing, almost afraid of being noticed. Her hands were perhaps a little too big for a woman and her chin perhaps a little too pointed, but the rest of her body was of proportions which would command admiration once it had succeeded in com-manding attention. She had a personality which could so easily be overlooked; but for those who stopped to take another look, the second look was bound to be a lingering one. In her relations with Hamisi, however, Salisha seemed particularly determined to be overlooked – almost as if she was afraid of what the second look might lead to.

She was at the moment oblivious of the fact that Hamisi was looking at her, first casually, then with growing puzzlement, and then with a deepening intensity and concentration. Had he seen her before? The past and the present, life before and life after, memory and forgetfulness – the world of Hamisi's consciousness was again misty, an interplay of vision and shadow, weird noises and pregnant silences. The booming voice of poetry again came through with the words:

> *And this is the crisis point,*
> *The twilight moment between*
> *sleep and waking;*
> *And voice that is reborn transpires,*

> *Not thro' pores in the flesh,*
> > *but the soul's back-bone.*
> *Hurry on down –*
> > *Thro' the high-arched gate –*
> *Hurry on down*
> > *little stream to the lake; ...*
> *Hurry on down*
> > *in the wake of the dream;*
> *Hurry on down – ...*

The voice had been getting louder and louder with each new imperative of *Hurry on down!* And in response, Hamisi was rising from his chair looking spellbound at Salisha – Hamisi was hurrying down towards the depths of recognition. The voice went on repeating like an obstinate refrain the commanding imperative downwards – until Hamisi screamed, 'I know those lines, Aisha, I know you, I know you!' Salisha looked up with despair in her eyes – with all the torment of reciprocated recognition!

For Hamisi the excitement was partly connected with the personality of Salisha herself, but also with the sheer psychological release of seeing someone he had known in the prior existence. Many of the things he had seen in this world were indeed only slightly different from similar things he had seen before. But Salisha was not a 'similar thing'. She was someone he had known, however briefly, in those yesteryears behind the grave.

'Aisha, Aisha, Aisha, Aisha! Why didn't you remind me? I have been so lost and bewildered.'

She had got up from her chair as he took steps towards her. He would have embraced her in the sheer ecstasy of psychological release, but she forced him back into a consciousness of his predicament by saying, 'Don't, Hamisi. You mustn't – I am Abiranja's companion.'

He stopped where he was, thrown into a state of indecision. Salisha gave him her hand and helped him back to his chair.

'Did you hear that voice? Did you hear the poetry?' Salisha had not heard it but she was wondering what to say to a man in a torment of hallucination and recognition, when the reality of his experience was suddenly revealed to her. For what he had heard was what must have plunged him into recognizing her. What he had heard was the missing link between the casual acquaintance in Abiranja's house beyond the grave and their night of weakness together in London many years before their deaths.

Hamisi was saying, 'I don't know whose voice it was, but the poetry I have been hearing in critical moments since I arrived here bears a definite identity. It is the poetry of Christopher Okigbo! Don't you remember, Aisha? It is the poetry of Christopher Okigbo!'

Yes, they remembered. They both remembered a single night . . . a lifetime ago.

4

It started as a Literary Night. Hamisi was at the time working for the B.B.C. African Service in London. He had been sent to London by the Kenya Broadcasting Corporation for training. Normally his work would have been oriented towards programmes intended for East Africa. But Hamisi's versatility and interest in literary matters gave him multiple functions in the B.B.C. African Service, and he was asked to take part in discussions ranging from a new development in Ghana and the place of cocoa-marketing in it, to the latest novel by Peter Abrahams. Hamisi's voice had become well known to B.B.C. listeners in West as well as in East Africa.

That night Hamisi was asked to interview Miss Aisha Bemedi, a Nigerian literary critic. The discussion was to start off with an evaluation of a new collection of poems by Christopher Okigbo.

Hamisi had not read much of Okigbo before, but as usual he set out to do his homework methodically a few hours before the programme. He read the new collection of poems which was to form the basis of the interview, at least at the beginning. He also looked up one or two other pieces by Okigbo which had appeared in magazines before. He noted that the poet was born in Ojoto in Eastern Nigeria in 1932, and took a degree in Classics at Ibadan University. Some critics were already proclaiming him to be the most gifted poet in the English language to have come out of Africa. Hamisi re-read some of the poems and jotted down notes in preparation for the interview with Miss Bemedi.

He looked up the information they had received about Miss Bemedi herself. At that time she was the only Northern Nigerian, of either sex, to have an M.A. in English; and she was the only Northern Nigerian woman to write publicly in magazines and take part in the cultural life of the new nation. Partly helped by the sense of uniqueness surrounding her situation, partly by the chivalry which successful women sometimes command from other intellectuals, and partly by her genuine ability as a literary critic, Miss Bemedi had made a significant impact in African and Negro magazines in different parts of the new world of black culture. Hamisi was quite flattered to be interviewing her. He was also intrigued to be discussing such matters with a Muslim woman. He made up his mind to take her out for dinner either immediately after the programme or on some other night in the near future.

When she turned up at Bush House, Hamisi's dating intentions were reinforced, for Miss Bemedi was a striking figure. She was dressed in a skirt and blouse, but wore in addition an embroidered *mtandio* to cover her hair and fall down elegantly across her shoulders. In the company of non-Muslims she often let the *mtandio* fall off completely to reveal the full intricacies of her North-African hairstyle. But she knew that her interviewer was to be Hamisi, and judging by his name if by nothing else, Hamisi must be a Muslim. Miss Bemedi's *mtandio* was therefore suitably in place as she announced her arrival to the receptionist on the floor of Bush House. Hamisi emerged a minute later with one of his captivating smiles, an arm extended in a great display of energetic welcome.

'Miss Bemedi – I am delighted you could come.'

The interview itself was one of the most successful that Hamisi had ever conducted. He soon found out that Miss Bemedi was a great admirer of Okigbo's poetry. To some extent Hamisi was surprised – partly because he expected political sensibilities to intrude and affect literary evaluations at this particular moment in Nigeria's history. As an East African he had a stereotyped image of relationships between Northern Nigerians and Southern Nigerians. He had also followed reports of political parties organized on the basis of regional and tribal affiliations. He expected women to be particularly susceptible to the broader socio-political conditioning factors of the society from which they sprang. But Miss Bemedi was sophistication itself. She seemed sincere in the ethos she propounded, that politics ought not to be allowed to interfere with aesthetic evaluations. She argued that political considerations had a host of subtle ways of entering the aesthetic domain. To disparage Okigbo's poetry because he was an Ibo poet was a crude political intrusion; but to praise Okigbo's poetry mainly because he was an African poet was, to Miss Bemedi, equally inadmissible. She argued that politics in contemporary Africa had manufactured a number of Trojan horses as a method of subtle invasion into kingdoms which should otherwise remain basically non-political. Enthusiasm for weak African writers simply because they were African was itself a Trojan-horse invasion by politics into aesthetics.

Hamisi suddenly realized that politics was also interfering in his interview with Miss Bemedi. He therefore diverted the discussion into a more direct evaluation of Okigbo's poetry. Hamisi, partly as a reaction to Miss Bemedi's enthusiasm, was rather negative in his judgements on Okigbo. He argued that Okigbo played with word pictures and word sounds without bothering to achieve a depth of poetic meaning. He cited lines that did not in themselves achieve intelligibility. Okigbo had a great gift for word-play, but not a great gift for poetry. Miss Bemedi heatedly denied the distinction between the two, arguing that great poetry depended on a highly developed sense of great word-play.

And so the conversation continued – claim and rebuttal, assertion and rejoinder, all on the place of meaning as opposed to imagery in the poetry of Okigbo. The two conversationalists in front of the microphone did not realize at the time what increased significance this particular issue would one day assume in a different setting, in a different world.

The red light that signalled the risk of an over-extended interview began to flicker. In the studio itself were only Aisha and Hamisi, but the big glass window by their side made them visible to the programme-director in the adjoining sound-proof room, and a machine operator who controlled the volume and flow of sound waves to B.B.C. listeners across the globe. When the red light flickered again, Hamisi turned his head a little to look at Godfrey, the director of interview programmes for the African Service of the B.B.C. Godfrey had two fingers up to denote that Hamisi had two more minutes with which to conclude the programme. Whereupon Hamisi said 'Thank you very much Miss Bemedi for a most stimulating defence of one of Africa's leading poetic talents. We pass on the great debate now to the listeners themselves to read and analyse afresh the lines of Christopher Okigbo . . . You have been listening to an evaluation of the latest collection of Okigbo's poems, a discussion between Miss Aisha Bemedi, the Nigerian literary critic, and your interviewer here at Bush House, B.B.C. London.'

Hamisi turned to look at Godfrey again who made a sharp move with his hand to denote that they were off the air now. Miss Bemedi and Hamisi sighed with relief – and as they did so their eyes met with a new nearness, having just shared tense moments of debate in front of a live microphone.

They left the studio and went into the sound-proof room for a minute, then emerged again into the corridor with Godfrey. Godfrey thanked Miss Bemedi warmly, and answering a query from Hamisi, confirmed that Hamisi was free until the following morning. As Hamisi was accompanying Miss Bemedi out of the Bush House complex, he was calculating on the best way of formulating a dinner invitation. He first offered to see her to the tube station, and then took the opportunity to start a whole new discussion on literature which he hoped Miss Bemedi would be reluctant to terminate too readily when they did get to the tube station. He had estimated her capacity for prolonged intellectual discussion quite accurately. It was true that when they got to the tube station, and Hamisi suggested a quick dinner at a nearby restaurant to complete the conversation, Miss Bemedi hesitated briefly; but she did after all have to have dinner somewhere before going for her German class at the Notting Hill Polytechnic that evening. After a short discussion on what kind of restaurant to go to, they decided on catching a tube after all – but in order to go to a special Chinese restaurant that Hamisi recommended strongly.

By the time they were having their meal, literary discussion had in fact receded into the background, giving way first to the politics of Nigeria and prospects for the survival of democratic and federal institutions, and then to a discussion comparing Muslim customs in Northern Nigeria and the coastal areas of East Africa. Both areas were highly orthodox in many ways; and both Hamisi and Miss Bemedi mused about the unlikelihood of a Muslim man and Muslim woman like themselves sharing an innocent meal together in a restaurant in Kano in Northern Nigeria, or in the biblical little town of Lamu along the eastern seaboard of the African continent.

Hamisi then managed to turn the conversation in a natural way to a discussion of African poetry in African languages. Specifically, upon mentioning Lamu, he proceeded to draw attention to the extraordinary impact of the dialect of this town on much of the classical poetry of the Swahili culture. Much of the classical Swahili poetry was in fact religious, in the same way that much of medieval art in Europe was church art. But the style of the Lamu dialect and its easy absorption of Arabic nuances, coupled with the verbal vivacity of the population, produced a poetic diction which animated the creative impulse in parts of the East African coast speaking vastly different Swahili dialects. Later on the effect of the Lamu dialect became adverse because it began to paralyse poetic forms. Experimentation was stultified and the diction of versified discourse became more and more artificial.

Nevertheless, Hamisi maintained, it was worth delving into such epics as *Utenzi Wa Mwana Kupona* or such magnificent pieces as *Inkishafi*. You could delve into these and sense some of the vibrant spirituality of their age, even in translation.

It was on the basis of this discussion of Swahili poetry in translation that Hamisi finally got round to inviting Miss Bemedi to his flat to look at some of the collections, both printed and manuscript, that comprised his personal library of East African literature.

It was 9.30 p.m. when they left The Rice Bowl. Miss Bemedi was a little uneasy about missing her German class. She was also a little uneasy about making a special trip to Ealing Broadway at that time of night, even for so good a cause as an examination of comparative literary pieces in East African languages.

As they left the restaurant to return to the tube station for a new destination something in Miss Bemedi was suppressed. It might have been her better judgement.

5

Hamisi's flat was not self-contained. He had to share a bath with other adjoining units in the same house. He had been careful about bringing women into his flat late at night, partly because the previous tenant had been a Ghanaian who over-indulged himself and was asked by the landlord to leave after an accumulation of complaints from his neighbours.

When they got to the house it was nearly half past ten. Ealing Broadway was after all quite a distance away, and the walk from the tube station took the best part of twenty minutes. Hamisi tried to open the little gate to the garden quietly, but that was a lost battle from the beginning. The gate always creaked. He took out his Yale key and opened the main door of the building. The staircase light was on, but there was no one in sight and the doors of the other flats were firmly shut.

'Come in,' Hamisi whispered to Miss Bemedi.

She went in, a little perplexed by the extra caution which Hamisi was taking to minimize the sounds of their entry, and yet somehow relieved since she was not sure she wanted to have witnesses who could affirm this particular magnitude of her literary interests. She herself did believe that her motivation on this trip was exclusively literary, and she was trusting enough to permit Hamisi a similar degree of honourable intent. But she sensed that the situation could so easily be misinterpreted by even the most well-meaning spectator.

They walked up the wooden staircase carefully, but by no means quietly. The steps had a way of squeaking a response of exultation to every tapping shoe.

However, they got to the door of Hamisi's flat completely unobserved. The key turned, the door opened. It was dark – but a darker arm penetrated the depths with confidence and a switch exposed each item in the room in the sudden brightness.

The flat was, in fact, a bed-sitter with a separate kitchen. The furniture was old, but Hamisi had items in the room which gave it extra dignity. There was a beautiful model of a dhow, carved in Lamu, which Hamisi had sent for after his first six months in England. It was brought to him by 'kind favour' of Abdul when he arrived to do his General Certificate of Education at Portsmouth. Another striking piece of furniture was an expensive radiogram, which Hamisi had obtained on hire purchase. It stood on an exquisite prayer-mat, probably of Persian origin. Hamisi had brought it with him from home for more devout purposes than it was now serving. There were also two Moroccan pouffes which Hamisi had stuffed with an accumulated collection of old issues of the *Mombasa Times* dutifully sent to him by a friend from home. The pouffes had been given to him by a departing Middle-Easterner who had been working for the B.B.C. Arabic Service.

Hamisi had a double bed, neatly made, with a silk-covered eiderdown protruding near the pillow from beneath a green bedcover.

The desk was the untidiest thing in the room. In the middle were two airletters half-written and awaiting final completion in Hamisi's moments of boredom. There was a portable typewriter in its cover on the floor underneath the desk. Two books and several copies of the B.B.C.'s monthly programmes for the African Service could be seen underneath a newly-arrived issue of the *Mombasa Times*.

Hamisi helped Miss Bemedi with her coat and put it neatly away in his wardrobe. He made her sit down and proceeded to enumerate the four types of alcohol that he had available. Miss Bemedi teasingly said that Hamisi should know better.

'I notice that you are a good Muslim in every way,' Hamisi reciprocated the teasing.

'No, not in every way! After all, I wouldn't be going out to dinner with strange men and visiting them at their flats at this hour of the night! But, I've so far resisted Western drinking habits. Alcohol on Muslim women has too great an effect – it corrodes and erodes away much of the Islamic upbringing!'

Hamisi doubted that. He argued that there was more to an Islamic personality than simple sobriety. He put the kettle on for coffee, shouting from the kitchen, 'Even I have retained one taboo – no bacon for breakfast!' They both laughed.

Setting to work on the overt main mission of that evening's visit to his flat, he brought out manuscripts of Swahili poetry – some written in Arabic script, some in Roman. Miss Bemedi was particularly intrigued by the usage of the Arabic alphabet for Swahili, and tried out her own knowledge of Arabic and Hausa as a guide to the pronunciation of some of the lines. It was an intriguing game while it lasted, but in due course, the main theme of their discussion reverted back to the style of Christopher Okigbo.

'Listen to these lines from the poet, Ali Rajabu,' exclaimed Hamisi. He read the lines about a black thread and a white thread whose distinctive identities lay suspended, awaiting revelation at dawn. 'Of course there is obscurity in these lines, but it is a different kind of obscurity from that which we find in Okigbo. Rajabu here is indeed revelling in sophisticated verbal obscurity. Enigmatic expressions, if properly handled, can be evidence of profundity.'

In the case of obscure passages from Rajabu, however, there

was such a thing as 'the *right* meaning' of a given line, and the task of the sophisticated reader was to discover that meaning. It was possible for a reader to be *wrong* about Rajabu.

'However,' continued Hamisi, 'the obscurity of abstract verse of Okigbo's variety is calculated to leave too much to the reader's imagination!' Hamisi picked up a magazine and quoted from Okigbo:

> *the only way to go*
> *through the marble archway*
> *to the catatonic pingpong*
> *of the evanescent halo . . .*

'Can there ever be a "*right* meaning" to such a passage?'

Miss Bemedi countered with the argument that the task of the poet was not to impose an interpretation of his own verse. Poetry was not a constitution to be debated by legalistic minds as to the meaning of this or that word. The business of the poet was not to tell, but to stimulate. The question of right and wrong meaning did not therefore arise.

Hamisi began to notice that he was getting too interested in the dialectical aspects of the evening and was arousing in Miss Bemedi only the formidable intellectual side of her personality. The task now was to divert her attention back to softer thoughts.

Therefore, the next point he chose to illustrate was neither an exercise in profundity nor a religious evocation. It was a teasing poem from Pate about a lover stealing his way into the thatched quadrangle of an aristocratic house. These were lines which, astonishingly enough, could also be a translation of the independently composed poetry of Robert Browning:

> *A tap at the pane, the quick sharp scratch*
> *And blue spurt of a lighted match,*
> *And a voice less loud thro' its joys and fears,*
> *Than the two hearts beating each to each!*

It was extraordinary that two poets, one in Pate, and one in London, both writing during the nineteenth century, without a connecting imperial link and with no conceivable possibility of inter-influence, should have captured an experience in lines which sounded strikingly similar, though written in different languages.

Then Hamisi drifted into illustrating poems which were intended to be danced – a fusion of mind and body, word and movement. He brought out a *leso*, a brightly patterned rectangular piece of cloth widely used in pairs by women along the coast of Kenya and Tanzania. One *leso* was used to cover the woman from the breast downwards, and the other to cover her from the breast upwards, keeping the face open but covering the hair when out of doors.

An additional *leso* might sometimes be used by a woman in the course of a dance. It would be tied tight around the hips to emphasize the movement of her buttocks in the tempestuous response of wiggling rhythm. Hamisi himself could wiggle beautifully as he illustrated the body's response to the drumming of the *msondo*. Miss Bemedi watched his movements and began to sense an awkward discomfort. The tight *leso* around his hips, the vibrations of his dance, the tightening masculinity which her eyes had to avoid. She was about to ask him to stop it, when suddenly he stopped himself. She got up, awkwardly seeking to pour herself another cup of coffee. She felt his hand on her shoulder, and the warmth of his breath as he said, 'You try the *leso* on – you dance to the *msondo!*'

He began to tie the *leso* around her waist. She had stopped breathing – and he knew it. He reached for her hand and guided her away. She followed with calm docility. Her coffee cup was half full, and cold. Cold too was the eiderdown as it slipped smoothly to the floor.

19

6

Salisha had found her way back to her chair. Hamisi was asking 'Why did you walk out of my life so completely? Why did you decree that not a single day would be added to that one night of ours?'

Salisha was silent for a little while. She had stopped knitting and she was looking rather blankly at a wall. Hamisi waited patiently for her response. It would have been easy to conclude that she had not heard a thing he said, but somehow Hamisi knew better. He just waited. Gradually Salisha turned her eyes away from the wall, the blankness in them had dissolved, and she looked at him.

'It was that half completed airletter on your desk!'

Salisha recalled the sudden compulsion she felt to read it. It might have been 5.30 in the morning; twilight had invaded the privacy of their night together. Hamisi was asleep by her side, exhausted by the tempest of that experience. He was naked. She was almost naked but not quite. She had covered her breasts out of a strange impulse of modesty.

Like Hamisi, she had dozed off for a while. But then she had woken up, and as consciousness continued she lay in deep communion with the silences of the night. She thought she loved this man, who in a single evening had torn away all the sophisticated self-protection which she had thought she possessed. In a single journey Hamisi had made a trip from total externality into the innermost chambers of her being. Who was this man? What was he?

It was while her mind was trying to piece together the identity of the naked man by her side that she suddenly remembered the unfinished letters on his desk. It was odd how memory had a way of throwing up impresssions, which at the time they were made could not have been more casual. As they had entered Hamisi's flat earlier that evening she had noticed a number of things: the arrangement of the furniture and the odd mixture of Westernism, Orientalism, and a residual Africanness in the collection of items which together constituted the personality of the room. Her eyes had also rested on the desk and she had noticed those uncompleted letters awaiting the renewed interest of their writer.

Now several hours later those letters flashed across her consciousness once again. At first they were simply a matter of passing interest as she contemplated the events of that evening and the situation in which she found herself. But gradually a strange mixture of anger and tender curiosity started mounting in intensity as her mind dwelt on her ignorance. How could she have capitulated to a total stranger in so short a time? It might not have been like being picked up in the street, but it was certainly like being picked up from a dance. It was so strange that a medium so public as a broadcast should have opened the gates into an experience as private as this bed. But why had she permitted the gates to open? And who was this stranger who had known where to strike, in spite of all her intellectual armoury? There was an irrepressible affection for him despite it all, but Miss Bemedi was getting more and more impatient with her own ignorance about him. She turned to look at him again in the twilight. It was extraordinary how peacefully men slept after their exertions. She could see the outline of his neck, the shoulder next to her, and half a masculine chest exposed to the cold airs of dawn beyond the blankets. She could no longer stand his blissful anonymity. Almost compulsively she shifted her position and started creeping out of the blankets. She touched him twice in the course of the operation. He groaned the second time and turned the other way. But he was still fast asleep. She got out and tiptoed towards the desk. Yes, the uncompleted letters were still there. She hesitated for a second and then reached for both of them. She simply had to find out something about him before she looked him in the eye when he woke up. She tiptoed to the window; the curtain was already letting in the twilight from outside, but the girl lifted one side of it a little more to admit extra light on to the dark paper she was holding. She knew that if the

21

letter was impersonal, addressed to a mere acquaintance, this violation by her of the simple canons of civilized behaviour would not be rewarded. A letter by a stranger to an acquaintance was hardly an exercise in self-revelation.

One of the airletters was addressed to a male friend of Hamisi's, starting quite simply with the words 'Dear Ali'. She strained hard to read the first paragraph of the incomplete letter. There was little else apart from an acknowledgement of a letter from Ali, and a casual comment on an item of gossip which Ali must have conveyed to Hamisi. The English was interlaced with Swahili expressions. Aisha Bemedi then turned to the other airletter. She felt cold and anxious. Curiosity on the one hand, and fear of knowledge on the other, struggled for supremacy in that split second, but victory for one side was swift – she strained to read the other airletter. She looked away quickly, unable to go on. In this case she could not bear to read the paragraph which followed the opening line. She had at one time thought of taking both notes into the kitchen, shutting the door, putting the light on and conducting this sneaky exploration in better light. But she suppressed the temptation under the disturbing impact of the opening line of the second airletter. And yet . . . and yet . . . what if the opening line had another explanation? She hesitated again, but began to accuse herself of wishful thinking. She had let herself drift into a night of intimacy with a shadowy figure from the external world. She was now beginning to build up on it and to see her whole future tied to this man. She had just seen evidence, that for him at any rate, such a night was all in a day's work – peripheral privileges accruing to working with the B.B.C.

With the quick decisiveness of which she was capable in moments of agitation, Miss Aisha Bemedi made up her mind to make an instant exit out of Hamisi's life. She got dressed in that twilight, half fearful that he might wake before she finished. She tried to be as quiet as possible, but she had an anxious moment when her left foot accidentally kicked the portable typewriter resting on the floor near the desk. But Hamisi slept soundly on. Towards the end of the operation, she had to open the curtains a little more in order to be able to see sufficiently well to accomplish her departure. She shut her handbag firmly and took a last lingering look at the outline of Hamisi in bed. She knew her hair was a mess as she prepared to leave, but that couldn't be helped. She opened the door softly and stepped out into the corridor. Before shutting it she took one last look into the room. She could hear Hamisi breathing peacefully. On the coffee-table, centrally placed to receive the light of dawn which came through the wider parting of the curtains, Aisha Bemedi saw for the last time the outline of one of the books on Swahili poetry and the unmistakable outline of the little volume of poems by Christopher Okigbo. She shut the door, stood for a second in the corridor, and then walked across to the top landing of the staircase. She thought of the squeaking wood down those stairs and of the neighbours in the flats below who had hounded Hamisi's Ghanaian predecessor out of the building altogether. She swallowed hard, held her handbag firmly and made her squeaking descent to the outside world. As she stepped into the garden and shut the outside door behind her, she though she heard the door of one of the flats inside fly open. It might have been her imagination. She opened the little gate of the garden and walked out into the early morning chill of that small London street.

'Yes, it was that uncompleted airletter which decided the issue,' Salisha said.

In the setting of another world, more than a decade after that night, Hamisi could not remember what that half-completed letter could have been. Who was it addressed to? Why was the opening line so devastating? And why, for heaven's sake, was Aisha Bemedi now bearing the name of Salisha?

Hamisi got up, excited at having had to relive that night all over again, agitated also at having had to re-experience the worried perplexity of that morning when he had opened his eyes only to see that his companion of the night had vanished with the darkness. Then followed the questions which were rephrasing themselves under the impact of additional information, and under the influence of a new universe, still inadequately grasped by him.

23

He was about to plead for further illumination when they heard the door open. Abiranja was back from his unknown mission with friends. Salisha, who had remained seated, got up. Abiranja looked worried as well as tired. And she worried with him.

He then broke the news. Christopher Okigbo had been killed in the Nigerian Civil War and had just arrived in After-Africa. Salisha waited; a cloud of fearful expectancy had cast a shadow on her.

'The Elders of After-Africa have arrested him on a high charge!' Abiranja completed the sad tidings from the depths of the night.

Salisha turned to look at Hamisi, tied to him by a poetic refrain from a previous lifetime. Hamisi looked puzzled and deeply moved. Suddenly, the voice began beaming lines of poetry again. Abiranja was changing into his slippers, evidently an outsider to the experience of that voice. He was not within reach of those soundwaves. But Salisha and Hamisi, looking into each other's eyes, seemed to be, for the first time in this new universe, joint hearers of the same mysterious recitation of Okigbo's poetry from the womb of the unknown:

> Before you, mother Idoto,
>   naked I stand;
> before your watery presence,
>   a prodigal
> leaning on an oilbean,
> lost in your legend.
>
> Under your power wait I
>   on barefoot,
> watchman for the watchword
>   at Heavensgate:
> out of the depths my cry:
> give ear and hearken . . .

7

There was not much of the night left when the news of Okigbo's arrival came with Abiranja. In any case Abiranja, Hamisi, and Salisha decided not to go to bed that night, but to think and talk about it all. Hamisi was inevitably the most perplexed as to the meaning of Okigbo's arrival and his arrest. Before long, however, he began to connect these events with a memorable line drawn from a conversation he had had with Abiranja: 'Death is an exercise in Pan-Africanism!' Hamisi began to sense that somehow the significance of all this excitement sprang from the womb of that single sentence.

But did it make sense to talk of 'arrest' in After-Africa? Was there a police force beyond the grave? Was there a judiciary to organize trials and pass sentences? In one form or another Hamisi raised some of these questions during what was left of that night, as part of a general conversation about the latest events in After-Africa.

'Yes, of course there is government in After-Africa,' affirmed Abiranja.

Hamisi wanted to know in what way it was connected with . . . again he hesitated. He swallowed hard and asked: 'Where does the old concept of God come into the governmental arrangements of After-Africa?'

Abiranja asserted that most religions in the Herebefore reduced heaven to a completely autocratic system. They assumed that what lay beyond the grave was the undiluted supremacy of the Almighty, sitting in judgement over his creatures with no ballot box, no jury. The so-called day of judgement was deemed to be a once-for-all affair of divine autocracy. Given such a conception of heaven, John Milton was right when he put it, in the words of Satan, *Better to reign in Hell than serve in Heaven*. Milton disapproved of Satan's rebellion against divine omnipotence, but he portrayed God as such a vainglorious king that the reader must at times be forced to agree and sympathize with Satan rather than God. Milton's Almighty sits on his throne enjoying perpetual hymns of praise from his angels and worshippers. The great sin of *Paradise Lost* is supposed to be the sin of human pride; yet the God portrayed in that poem is divine vanity personified. And if man is indeed created in the image of God, pride might be thought to be a modest approximation to the vanity of the King who sits listening to endless hymns in his own praise from fervent worshippers.

At first Hamisi's religious feelings were somewhat disturbed by Abiranja's denunciation of earthly concepts of God. It was true that Milton's *Paradise Lost* was portraying the God of Christian mythology; but it was not at all certain that Islam's *Allah* was not at least as hyper-regal and demanding.

But what Abiranja was denouncing was not the idea of God itself, but certain ideas of God's behaviour and God's personality which were popular in the Herebefore. In reality, heaven was not an autocratic regime, but included the participation of the residents of heaven, who were the living dead. Abiranja insisted that God did not just sit on his throne administering penalties and rewards, but permitted these human beings, not fewer rights than they had enjoyed in a less perfect world before the grave, but more rights and liberties. Democracy in heaven could not but include a high degree of participation by the living dead in the affairs of their own communities. Sentences were not simply passed by one omnipotent judge, but permitted the utilization of human juries, human assessors, and indeed human judges. Great trials were subject to the jurisdiction of nine human Elders. God had the ultimate prerogative of mercy, but much of the rest of the process of justice was firmly in the hands of the living citizenry beyond the grave. What was important in After-Africa was the continental dimension and the boundaries of jurisdiction of this entire process. Offences were offences of the region, and the ethos which guided the administration of justice was a regionally distinctive ethos. For ease of organization, as Abiranja had indicated before, the world beyond the grave had not dispensed with geography. Continental boundaries remained to lend ease of definition to the concept of community after death.

'But where does the arrest of Christopher Okigbo fit into all this?' asked Hamisi.

Abiranja explained that every major upheaval in Africa had its repercussions in After-Africa. One obvious repercussion lay in the number of people who died in a particular convulsion in Africa.

'Look at that shield,' said Abiranja, pointing at the wall opposite. 'That was Chaka's immense shield in one of the battles. In the Zulu wars thousands of casualties came to the gates of After-Africa, and there were three major trials of people connected with those wars.'

One of the accused was from another continent, and so After-Africa had had to send a special inter-continental demand of arrest. The continents after death did have a system of extradition, repatriation, and inter-jurisdictional arrests. A culprit in After-Europe wanted for an offence committed in Africa in the Herebefore could be sent for by the authorities of After-Africa in friendly communication with After-Europe. Cecil Rhodes, for example, was a case of inter-jurisdictional transfers and stood trial in After-Africa for offences committed upon Africa in the Herebefore. Warren Hastings was demanded by After-Asia for trial, although the House of Lord in old England had acquitted him. Sometimes people who were not in the public eye in life before the grave had become critical personalities after the grave for offences committed in the Herebefore. Confidential agents, spies generally, secret assassins in situations which later burst forth into catastrophe, had on occasions become the focus of dramatic trials after death.

'Nor must it be assumed,' Abiranja continued, 'that those who are made to stand trial are necessarily those who directly caused the greatest upheavals in the Herebefore. Human beings in the world before the grave sometimes misunderstand the real causes of their own convulsions, and mistake the passing prominence of a particular historical figure for the real causes behind a particular

27

historical event. Sometimes kings, princes, presidents, and generals are more incidental as causes behind great events than journalists and historians in the Herebefore have often assumed.

'Those who are picked for trial are sometimes just symbols of wider phenomena, or are igniting instruments in situations which were already latently combustible. The trial of the killer of Frances Ferdinand, for example, was a case in point. One of the immediate causes of the First World War in the Herebefore was supposed to be the assassination of the heir to the Austrian throne, the Archduke Frances Ferdinand, in 1914. After-Europe, while recognizing the incidentality of the assassination as a factor in the European explosion of 1914-18, decided nevertheless to bring the assassin before a panel of judges after death. To some extent the trial was not of the assassin of the Archduke, but was a trial of Europe as a whole.'

Abiranja then referred to the Congo situation soon after independence. The death of Lumumba had indeed caused a diplomatic convulsion in the Herebefore. But there were few ripples in After-Africa. The really important trial in After-Africa connected with the Congo was that of an unknown mutineer in the Force Publique who had helped in sparking off the military insurrection soon after Belgian withdrawal, and set loose the torrents of anarchy in that country. The Elders in After-Africa decided to have this particular mutineer arrested immediately on arrival beyond the grave, and the mutineer was judged both for himself, and as an embodiment of the guilt or possible innocence of the Congo as a whole.

Hamisi was beginning to see the place of Christopher Okigbo in all this. The Nigerian Civil War had shaken Africa at least as profoundly, as ever the Congo troubles had done a few years previously. Thousands of Africans had been forced to trek on the highroad to infinity. Mass arrivals into After-Africa were something akin to the inflow of refugees from unhappy lands. Problems of adjustment beyond the grave were compounded. To use the language of the Herebefore, the ancestors were deeply disturbed by the turn of events in Nigeria.

Hamisi looked out of the window. Daylight was creeping back. It was itself like an invading army pushing back the dark resistance of the forces of night. The world of sight and vision was a battlefield for an eternal civil war between shadows and rays, darkness and light. Dawn and dusk were the great moments of confrontation when one army would assert control and the other retreat. But defeat was transient and victory was cyclic.

'Yes, it's morning,' Salisha was saying.

8

They took Hamisi to a football match that Friday. Hamisi was relieved to know that some of these old forms of entertainment were still available in life beyond the grave.

'Yes, of course,' said Abiranja laughing, 'the only difference is that the choice of games here is vastly increased. Not only do men from different parts of old Africa teach each other their own sub-regional games, but men from different centuries reveal to their new friends the forms of entertainment which their own time enjoyed and which might later have gone out of fashion. Such games can easily be revived in this after-life if they are enjoyable.'

Abiranja went on to add that sometimes games from later centuries were propagated among citizens who came from prior ones. 'Take today's match, for example. It is, as I mentioned earlier, a match between the Eleventh Century in Africa and the Sixteenth Century in Africa. Well, soccer was not invented at that time anywhere in the world. In fact, it found its way into Africa as a result of imperial rule. Yes, the twentieth century arrivals into After-Africa quickly managed to fire the imagination of the rest of us with the attraction of this particular game. The British in Africa-before-the-grave were themselves astonished at the rapid success of soccer among African societies at large. Well, they would be even more astonished if they knew of the extent to which it has conquered After-Africa.' They all laughed at this.

The stadium where the match was being played was a striking structure of marble pillars rising upwards to meet a plain but vast dome. But the sky shone also all around those pillars. The football-ground was a magnificence of natural green carpetry. The grass was cut with an evenness which was almost mathematically determined. The goalposts might have been wooden, but from a distance they, too, looked like marble, standing in narrow majesty with the net spreading forth behind them, like a royal robe descending in perfect symmetry from the height of the cross-bar.

The crowd seemed limitless in size. Hamisi had never seen anything like it. In magnitude the crowd must have been the equivalent of several Olympic Games put together. Most of the men were in *kanzus*, and most of the women in that black neo-Punjabi dress with a white border. Each sex was in uniform, but together they comprised a diform of alternating patterns when seen as a multitude from the other side of the stadium. Until the game started, the place buzzed and hummed with the sound of thousands of individual conversations. It occurred to Hamisi quite accurately that what he was listening to was the sound of several centuries in instant communication with each other. Man and man, across decades and generations, were in discourse at a football match.

The match itself was a knock-out game. The Eleventh Century of Africa had been doing extremely well, having already knocked out of the competition the Tenth, Twelfth, Thirteenth, Fourteenth, and Fifteenth centuries. They had learnt the game of soccer with a proficiency and zest which would stun the current practitioners of this art in the Herebefore.

At 4.30 there was a spontaneous and deafening burst of applause as the team of the Eleventh Century entered the arena. In many ways the reaction was not very different from what it might have been at a football-match in Nakivubo Stadium in Kampala or at Wembley with Manchester United as the favourites. There was general excitement – whistling, clapping and the vibration of outbursts of collective exultation.

Members of the Eleventh Century stood in their positions, from

30

the goalkeeper to the centre forward, awaiting the challengers. Hamisi, who had been startled when they first appeared, remained intrigued by the fact that the whole team was stark naked but for a girdle of red beads around the waist of each player. Again there was a majesty in those eleven black bodies standing erect and proud in the afternoon sun, the centre forward with his foot on the ball at the centre of the stadium, awaiting the competitors.

A couple of minutes later another burst of applause shook the stadium as the rival team entered the arena. They, too, were stark naked, but around the waist of each was a girdle of white beads. Their supporters thumped in exhilaration as they, in turn, took their position, spaced out with precision and order from the goal-keeper, the backs, the wings, the outside left and the outside right, the inside left and the inside right, to the regal centrality of the forward man.

Hamisi wondered why he could see the players so clearly from so far back in the stadium. He later found out that the structure of the stadium had been so planned that the interplay of light on the football field itself always afforded maximum visibility and clarity of vision. There were also two huge artificial lights hanging high above each end of the stadium. When they were on they gave extra magnification to the size of the players in proportion to their distance from the spectator. To no spectator was the player bigger than life, but to none was the player much smaller than life either. The process of magnification was a visual aid which increased in effectiveness only as you moved backwards away from the centre of the stadium. The appearance of naturalness in the size, bearing, and colour of the players was never lost.

While they were waiting for the referee to start the match, Hamisi learned that there had been a time when each team was required to turn up at the arena in a mode of dress most representative of its century. But this idea was discarded quite early. In the first place, several centuries in Africa had been known to encompass the same collection of modes of attire with little or no variation, and since the football matches were often organized on the basis of one century against another, there were always problems in centuries too close together in Africa's experience. A second difficulty was the position taken by several African communities whose civilization had never been convinced of the utility of dress in hot and uncomfortable climates. Again, civilizations of this kind were scattered throughout every age of African history. A third difficulty concerned the weight of some of the modes of attire of particular periods and regions. Some, more like togas and robes, were hardly calculated for easy movement in a soccer game. Others, consisting of animal skins and hides, were sometimes impressive without being convenient.

The Sporting Association of After-Africa therefore decided quite early in the after-history of organized sports that complete and natural nakedness was the most rational attire for competitive exertions. But nakedness, while revealing the full physical identity of the individual player, was bound to blur the identity of the collective group. It was because of this factor that the device of a girdle of coloured beads around the waist of each player was devised as a uniform to differentiate one team from the other. And there they were now down there, the red beads against the white, the Eleventh Century against the Sixteenth.

Suddenly, the whistle went. A deep hush descended for a split second; then the match started. There was an air of leisureness at first as the players of the Eleventh Century exchanged greetings with the ball from one part of the field to another. But the left back of the Sixteenth Century managed to get the ball, dodged the challenges of three opponents, and sent it spinning to the right wing of his team half-way across the field. The initiative from then on was with the white beads. The Eleventh Century found itself in a chronic state of defensiveness. Their goalkeeper was magnificent. In a swift move through the air he startled the spectators with a magnetic grip of the ball which, with a spinning ferocity, had appeared uncontrollable on its way to the net. The goalkeeper also had a tremendous felicity with his fist, and accomplished a crucial diversion of the direction of the ball several times by the brave use of his clenched right hand. The centre half of the Eleventh Century also put up quite a show, at times appearing almost like an impenetrable fortress. But when the ball did get past him the glory of the defence of the red beads reverted once again to the swift movements of the goalkeeper. For most of the first half of play, the ball was defiantly on the red beads' side of the ground. The stadium vibrated with collective bursts of admiration, for both the swift gamework in the offensive of the challenging team, and the startlingly effective defences of the red champions.

It was just before half-time when the Sixteenth Century scored a goal. Hamisi would never forget that tumultuous explosion which burst forth from the people. The crowd simply went mad with all the power of pent-up expectancy. The shouting, the clapping, the whizzing gadgets of the younger members of the crowd, the *vigele gele* of the women! The whole stadium was heaving with excitement. The goal itself had been the result of almost mathematical teamwork. The ball had passed from the inside right to the left wing who dodged the attack of the right back of the opposition as well as of their inside right. He then passed it swiftly, level to the ground, to his own centre forward. The centre forward ran with it like a racing stallion towards the goal of the red team. He could have scored the goal himself, and almost everyone expected him to make the attempt. But precisely because all expectations had focused on his next move, he decided on a surprise. He could once again see the left wing of his team strategically placed and in readiness to act if he was called upon to do so. The brilliant goalkeeper of the red team was himself restlessly changing from one position to another awaiting the kick from the centre forward. But the kick was not in his direction. With a breathtaking diversionary move, the centre forward shot the ball to the left wing, and before the crowd or the goalkeeper could regain breath, the leftwinger had sent the ball swiftly home. It was this network of events which, when the goal came, had shaken the stadium into a mad frenzy.

Now the two teams were standing again in position after the goal, their naked bodies glistening in the afternoon sun. It was as

33

if they had all just emerged from ancestral huts where their limbs had been massaged with fresh and smooth coconut oil. Their chests heaved with a mixture of fatigue and suppressed fear. The men in the crowd looked on; the women watched. The whistle went and the game started again.

It was about this time that a man came to where Hamisi, Abiranja, and Salisha were standing. They did not hear his footsteps. He patted Abiranja on the shoulder. Abiranja turned round and the two went off together. Half-time came and Abiranja was still not back. But he did turn up in the course of the second half of the game. He said to Salisha, 'I must go away again with Solomon. Have your dinner with Hamisi and don't wait for me. But I don't think I will be very late.'

Abiranja looked at Hamisi in a strange way, almost as if he were sizing him up or trying to understand him. For a minute Hamisi wondered whether it had anything to do with the past relationship between him and Salisha. Did Abiranja know about it? And what was his own relationship to the girl?

Just at this minute the crowd exploded again. They all turned round to look at the field. This time it was a narrow save for the white challengers as the ball hit the bar, set it vibrating, and missed the net by a fraction of an inch.

Hamisi turned round again. Abiranja was gone.

9

The multitude poured out of the stadium like the first gush of a diverted Tigris. Hamisi put his arm round Salisha in an instinctive move of protection. The soccer match had been a powerful experience. Never since he came to After-Africa had he received such a clear indication of the massive cumulation of humanity that inhabited this part of human consciousness. The match between the Eleventh and the Sixteenth Centuries had been witnessed by several million spectators, drawn from several centuries of Africa's historical existence. The stadium had looked vast, and yet some-how even the remotest spectator had seen every naked player in the right human proportions of his being. The tumult of response towards every dramatic move was itself a phenomenon. Layer upon layer of perception, drawn from generations of beings who had trodden the soil of the African continent, gasped at every dramatic move in the course of the game. They used to say in the Herebefore that the distinctive thing about African social life was the centrality of collective experience. The solidarity of the vil-lage and the bonds of kinship provided the framework for much of this experience. Whether this was true in the Herebefore was something about which Hamisi was not clear in his present stage of reorientation. But the football match had demonstrated a different kind of collective depth. If death was an exercise in Pan-Africanism, that soccer game which Hamisi had just witnessed was definitely an improvement over an OAU conference. United across several centuries the dead of Africa had just been sharing two hours of living sport.

Hamisi and Salisha walked silently for a while, as the liquified humanity from the stadium poured forth on either side of them in torrential excitement. The Sixteenth Century had won the match with that single goal. It was a bitter experience for the Eleventh Century, after all the victories they had had. And yet it added a lot to the excitement of the football season of After-Africa to have such victors at last vanquished.

Hamisi was wondering why the Sixteenth Century had more than once denied itself the opportunity of scoring an additional goal. They had come pretty near to a devastating opportunity, only to shrink back from taking advantage of it. There seemed to be a certain purpose in this act of self-denial, and Hamisi was not clear as to its meaning.

The crowds had now thinned a lot, and familiar landmarks were beginning to command even Hamisi's attention. But he was curious about that aspect of the game, and he raised the issue with Salisha.

Salisha explained that in the first few hours of a game as played in the land of After-Africa both teams were engaged in a desperate attempt to establish what Salisha called 'a monotheistic lead'. The ultimate ambition was to separate oneself from one's opponents by a single goal. In the first few minutes of a game therefore, attack was the imperative. But once the goal had been scored, the victorious team then shifted its entire strategy to defence. The commitment was a commitment against equalization. A small margin of superiority by one team over the other was supposed to be aesthetically more satisfying than a wider measure of separation.

But the defeated team had to attempt equalization whatever happened. If the defeated team succeeded in establishing parity with its opponents, both teams resumed attack as the strategy of action on the field. Both teams became once again engaged in the relentless pursuit of a 'monotheistic lead'. The lead was still monotheistic if one side had two goals to its credit and the other had one. But a totality of three goals was at a lower level of purity than the single goal match. What Hamisi and Salisha had witnessed was the realization of the single goal model. The excitement of the crowds as they poured out of the stadium was intricately connected with this narrowness of margin in victory, and the purity of oneness in it all.

Salisha then took Hamisi in the direction of the open sea. Children were playing on the sand and many elderly people were sitting on those shadowy benches of primordial solidity. Was the sea the Atlantic? The Indian Ocean? The Mediterranean? The idea of trinity once again intruded into Hamisi's consciousness. Africa bounded by three major oceans, a unitary island on a trinity of water. But the colour of the water that Hamisi witnessed was somewhat different from the hue and texture of *Pwaa ya Liwali* on the shores of Mombasa. Here in After-Africa the sea had an extra depth of calmness and yet was not bereft of the crests of atavistic wave formation.

Hamisi told Salisha about his first initiation into the arts of the seas. He had swallowed a lot of salt water in Mombasa when some older playmates of his had forced him to fend for himself for a brief period. He had hated it to begin with, and yet could not remain ignorant indefinitely. The dangers had their own moments of excitement. He subjected himself again and again to moments of humiliation as he tried desperately to float, deeply mixed with feelings of panic and terror, that were somehow mitigated in their paralysing effect by the courage of activated determination to survive. A small creature from the land was learning the art of momentary survival in water. They had stripped by the side of *Pwaa ya Liwali*, leaving their shirts and shorts on the rocks, and ran in glistening nakedness towards the ripples. Where the sand ended and the water began one sometimes saw the equivalent of a horizon inverted and hammered out. What was once the meeting-point between the sky and the sea was now a meeting-point between the sea and the land.

Hamisi then asked Salisha whether there was an initiation into the life of After-Africa comparable to what creatures of the land experienced as they were initiated into the mysteries of survival in water.

'Yes,' Salisha said, 'sooner or later when we come into After-Africa we are called upon to pass the boundary. Much of African life in the Herebefore assumed the validity of *rites de passage*. The move from one stage of life to another involved a legitimizing initiation. Sometimes it was circumcision, and sometimes alternative modes of ceremonial admission into a new stage of existence. From generation to generation, from one status to another, Africa had its ways of opening the gates.'

Salisha was silent for a little while, and Hamisi did not press her to continue. He had a feeling that an important revelation about things to come was imminent in those casual exchanges.

'Death itself in many of our societies, you will remember, was one more ceremonial transition. It constituted a passing in some ways no more fundamental, and certainly no less fundamental, than the transition from pre-adulthood to the full status of the adult. Death was not an interruption but a continuation. And so here you are, Hamisi.'

Hamisi was not sure about the validity of this last statement. In

37

some important ways death had been an interruption. Yet all the same, there he was, Hamisi, with a girl with whom he had shared a moment of intimacy in the Herebefore.

Hamisi asked, 'But surely death should have been the last *rite de passage*. We moved from childhood to minimal adulthood, from minimal adulthood to married adulthood, and those who lived longer in the Herebefore went on to old age. Just as the adults were to be more revered than the adolescents, and just as the married ones deserved greater respect than those in pre-marital incompleteness, and just as the elderly commanded, in Africa, greater reverence than the younger ones, so were the dead to command greater mystique than the living. Each stage on the highroad of the journey of life was a moment of enhancement added to what had been before. All this I realize. But what, Salisha, is the stage after the enhancement of death?'

Salisha explained that those who had lived long in the Herebefore continued to have a margin of mystique in this world which followed. The elders of Africa, having died old, retained the credentials for extra consideration in the existence which followed. But the inequalities between generations and the privileges accruing to each were transformed after death. There was less rigidity in the distribution of privileges, and although After-Africa did not approve of total equality, it did approve of the ethic of minimal disparities.

Salisha continued to say that in addition to the narrowing differentials, and the residual reverence accruing to age in the Herebefore, there was an important final transitional stage to be undergone. This was the move from the state of being deceased to a state of being immortal. Abiranja was already an immortal. But Hamisi was still no more than a person deceased. A *rite de passage* was needed to enable him to be promoted from the status of the merely dead to the status of the immortal.

'When will I have to undergo this particular ceremony?' asked Hamisi.

'For all you know you may be undergoing it now. You are never told specifically what the test is you are undergoing. The

38

elders decide what awaits you, and the precise nature of the challenge. And then if you pass the challenge you move on to the new level of gradation.'

Hamisi was a little perplexed. He could not understand how the initiation ceremony could be so unspecified, and so unrelated to the conscious will of the person concerned as to be conceivably happening right at that moment to him. He asked Salisha for further explanation.

'Readiness is readiness without notice,' Salisha said. 'In Africa young men had notice about circumcision, and heard from quite early on what it entailed. I realize that Muslims on the East Coast were sometimes circumcized as babies, in the Islamic and Judaic tradition. For Muslims of the East Coast of Africa, masculine completeness necessitated the removal of unnecessary layers on the penis.'

Hamisi blinked. Such blunt language from an African woman of Salisha's sophistication was disconcerting. Salisha smiled.

'I see that you still have the inhibitions of the Herebefore. The Hereafter is decidedly post-Victorian!'

She continued, 'Anyhow, the main thing to grasp is that with some of our societies in the Herebefore, circumcision was masculine enhancement through phallic reduction. The male organ had to have a little bit of itself taken away, so that the male person could add something more to his status. Circumcision was the paradox of strength through reduction. It was also a form of physical undressing. By stripping it of the additional layer of skin, the organ was being undressed. It was therefore the less unready.'

Hamisi blinked again. He swallowed audibly, and Salisha once again flashed him an amused smile. It was in some ways fascinating that such a modest woman could also attain such levels of explicitness. But it was important that Hamisi should understand the wider context of the initiation from the ranks of the deceased to the status of immortality. As she had indicated, he might be undergoing the ceremony right at that moment.

10

Hamisi and Salisha were now approaching their neighbourhood As they entered the main street, and their house came into view, they saw Abiranja and Solomon standing at the door, seemingly waiting for them. The sense of expectancy was so obvious that Hamisi and Salisha found themselves instinctively hurrying. Abiranja came forward to meet them. He looked first at Salisha, and seemed to be communicating something to her. Hamisi was tense with anxious curiosity.

'Do come in, Hamisi,' said Abiranja. 'Solomon has come with important news that you will want to hear as quickly as possible.'

They went into the house. Solomon was leading the way, and Hamisi noticed the startling scar on the back of Solomon's neck. The man was almost more impressive to look at from behind than from the front, and the scar added a dimension to the personality of the man as a whole. They sat down. There was a moment of silence, pregnant with expectancy. Solomon gave an imperceptible nod to Abiranja, who then drew his chair a little closer and addressed Hamisi.

'I told you yesterday that Christopher Okigbo, the poet, had arrived in After-Africa. He was killed in the Nigerian Civil War and is now awaiting trial.'

Hamisi waited. He could see that Okigbo's arrival in After-Africa was an event of great significance, but what precisely that significance was somehow continued to elude him. Nor could he understand why Abiranja was reviving this subject of Okigbo's arrival in a manner which asserted its supreme relevance for Hamisi himself. Hamisi swallowed.

'Okigbo is to stand trial.'

Hamisi remembered the statement that death was an exercise in Pan-Africanism. He wondered whether Okigbo's trial was to be based on charges of betraying Pan-Africanism. He heard himself expressing a question, almost unconsciously.

'Does After-Africa regard secession as a crime? Is Okigbo's trial to be symbolic of this issue hanging over Africa itself in the Here-before?'

'It is true that there is an imperative of oneness underlying some basic values this side of the grave,' Abiranja explained. 'Both Pan-Africanism and monotheism share that imperative. The oneness of God and the oneness of Africa, both claiming moral indivisibility. No doubt the imperative of oneness is bound to feature in the trial of Christopher Okigbo. But that is not the main charge.'

Here Abiranja turned to Solomon. The vibrant voice of Solomon carried the explanation a stage further. 'Like most cases which come before the Elders, Okigbo's case concerns the distortion of values. He is to be charged with the offence of putting society before art in his scale of values.'

There was a moment of silence as Hamisi tried to absorb this statement. The charge had a quality of startling unexpectedness. Coming with his own earthly presuppositions still within his mental equipment, Hamisi had all too readily assumed that the real issue at work was between the claims of tribal loyalties as against the claim of national cohesion. But the charge put before him sounded, in some sense, bizarre – certainly esoteric. The anguish of puzzlement must have revealed itself in his eyes, for Solomon went on to clarify further.

'Okigbo gave his life for the concept of Biafra. As it happens that was a mortal concept, transient to his inner being. The art of a great poet, on the other hand, carries the seeds of immortality. No great artist has a right to carry patriotism to the extent of destroying his creative potential. The prosecution is going to suggest that Okigbo had no right to consider himself an Ibo patriot first, and an African artist only second. That was to subordinate the interests of generations of Africans to the needs of a collection of Ibos at an isolated moment in historical time.'

Hamisi struggled in his mind for a gleam of adequate comprehension. Was this a problem of ethics or aesthetics? Perhaps there was no difference between the two in the world beyond the grave. Aesthetic imperatives and moral dictates made a cohesive whole. He still thought the charges that were being considered so critical amounted to esoteric impulses. Yet there was no doubt that the arrival of Christopher Okigbo in After-Africa had been widely regarded as an occasion of momentous implications. When Abiranja had first announced the arrival of Okigbo, he announced it in a tone which implied an emergency of continental dimensions – a moment of anguish of self-evaluation for After-Africa as a whole. Abiranja had announced it in a manner which, in the Herebefore, would have signified a banner headline.

Certainly an even greater emergency, personal to himself, was sensed by Hamisi. He remembered in a startling moment of clarity that ever since he had gathered himself up from the railway tracks, he had moved in this world of the Hereafter amid echoes of poetry which at first he did not understand, but which later he recognized as Christopher Okigbo's. That was a long time before he ever heard that Okigbo had died. It was probably before Okigbo had in fact died. For some reason the echoes of his poetry, unsolicited, had forced their way into his subconscious repeatedly since he rose from the dead. Why had he been chosen? Why had those echoes disturbed the numbed recesses of his earthly memory? What did it all mean? What was it all about? And as he sought answers to these questions that familiar concentration of sound waves suddenly gripped the atmosphere. Solomon's face began to fade, shadows replaced the weighty presence of Abiranja, and even Salisha seemed to dissolve into thin visuality as the voice reciting poetry once again filled the room for Hamisi:

> For he was a shrub among the poplars,
> Needing more roots
> More sap to grow to sunlight,
> Thirsting for sunlight,

A low growth among the forest.

Into the soul
The selves extended their branches,
Into the moments of each living hour,
Feeling for audience

Straining thin among the echoes;

And out of the solitude
Voice and soul with selves unite,
Riding the echoes,

Horsemen of the apocalypse;

And crowned with one self
The name displays its foliage,
Hanging low

A green cloud above the forest.

It was not clear if anyone else had heard that voice. But Hamisi sat up electrified, sensing more than ever the ominous significance of this intrusion into his subconscious. Why had Christopher Okigbo's poetry been haunting him since he rose from the dead? Why had it disturbed him even before Okigbo himself had joined the ranks of the deceased?

With even greater tenseness, he started wondering why Solomon and Abiranja had with such solemnity sought to explain to him what the coming of Christopher Okigbo into After-Africa really meant. Why had they talked in such excited terms at the football match when Solomon came to fetch Abiranja? Why had the two men been waiting with earnest expectancy at the door as Hamisi and Salisha approached the house after the soccer match? Why had they seated him with such serious intentness and made him the centre of a session of explanation? Somehow, in ways which he could not fathom, he was at the heart of the drama.

'Did you hear that voice reciting poetry?' he heard himself inquiring.

No, he had been the only one privy to a dialogue with a primordial emptiness.

'Now please explain where I come into it. Why am I the centre of this attention in relation to the trial of Christopher Okigbo?'

Abiranja looked at Solomon. He then looked at Salisha. She seemed tense. The moment had come to define a destiny. Solomon did it with startling brevity.

'You, Hamisi, have been elected to defend Christopher Okigbo before the Elders against the charges in question.'

Hamisi saw himself standing up immediately, only half-aware that he did so.

'I? I defend Chris Okigbo? But I hardly know the man! I do not understand the charges in spite of what you have said. I do not understand the system of trial and defence. I haven't a clue what it is all about. Elected to defend Okigbo? By whom?'

He started pacing about the room, his fists clenched. He could not believe it.

Salisha got up, concerned, and to some extent shocked by the news. Hamisi turned to look at her. His eyes sought comfort. They were also seeking a reprieve from agonizing perplexity.

Salisha went to him, caught hold of his hand, and guided him back to his chair. She did not say a word. He sat down obediently and waited. Solomon continued.

'The Elders in their wisdom have selected you to be Counsel for Salvation. This is the equivalent of what in some earthly legal traditions was called Counsel for the Defence. I am not quite sure why the Elders chose you. It is at once a great opportunity and a great risk. If things go well you could become, in spite of your age, a future candidate for the status of an Elder in a judicial position. That would be high honour indeed. But if you make a mess of the brief, certain unpleasant consequences might follow. It depends upon the precise nature of the mishap. Different failures entail different painful repercussions.'

Hamisi remembered the discussion about initiation. Salisha had indicated that initiation could consist of almost any enterprise, sometimes not even the obvious. To be Defence for Salvation in a major trial sounded like a rather obvious type of initiation. But it was also immensely complimentary in its very dimensions. What had Salisha indicated about the nature of initiation? She had said that the circumcision ceremony in Africa in the Herebefore was, for Muslims like himself on the Eastern seaboard, an exercise in masculine enhancement. But he knew that among other tribes and communities the circumcision ceremony was more than masculine enhancement in the sexual sense. It was also a test of masculinity in the sense of physical courage. The ultimate defining organ of manliness was subjected, not to the pleasurable sensations for which it was biologically intended, but to the sharp incision of a razor. To experience this without flinching was an ideal to which no one really attained; but to experience it without screaming was a more manageable aspiration.

11

Solomon had left. Abiranja and Salisha were to explain further the implications of the assignment so dramatically entrusted to Hamisi. Hamisi had not had a legal training. He had had a relatively limited acquaintance with judicial processes, even in the Herebefore. His participation in panel discussions for the B.B.C. in London might have helped to sharpen his powers of argument and debating skills, but of the law itself, either beyond or prior to the grave, he knew very little.

Abiranja admitted that this might be the actual test for the transition from the ranks of the dead to the status of an immortal, but this did not necessarily follow. The Elders sometimes elected people to undertake particular assignments with no special reward in mind, and with no special penalty in prospect should the job not be well done. But it was extremely unusual for a new arrival in After-Africa to be entrusted with such a momentous job

– and it would certainly be unusual if the job was completely unrelated to the requirements of initiation.

What Abiranja emphasized was that if it was connected with initiation, the test need not necessarily be whether Hamisi won the case or not. This would make the whole exercise a little too obvious, and initiation ceremonies in the Hereafter were partly based on the conception of readiness as against preparation. Readiness implied a constancy without the necessity of warning; preparation suggested prior anticipation and planning.

'I am not saying that the challenge intended has nothing to do with the issue of winning the case,' Abiranja was clarifying. 'Certainly if you won the case, your whole future career in After-Africa could be decisively changed for the better. But the Elders may not necessarily be looking for qualities of ultimate triumph, but more for qualities related to handling specific problems. You could lose the case and still display positive qualities of the kind demanded by a specified situation.'

Salisha asked Abiranja whether it was known as yet who was going to be Counsel for Damnation. Hamisi inferred that this was the equivalent of the earthly Prosecutor. If Hamisi was going to be Counsel for Salvation it was important to know the kind of man with whom he would be engaged in a battle of debate and wits. Abiranja said he hoped the contests awaiting Hamisi would not be too severe. It was a polite way of saying that he hoped the Counsel for Damnation was not too intelligent and skilful for poor Hamisi.

How much time did they have? Abiranja told Hamisi that he had a single week in which to think out his case, try to grasp the judicial system of After-Africa, assess modes of potential impact in the debating arena, and brief himself fully about the Nigerian situation, the Civil War, and the life of Christopher Okigbo.

A single week! Hamisi felt so cold. Memories came gushing forth of hectic nights on the eve of examinations at the Polytechnic in London. He also recalled a desperate hour or two trying to organize a broadcasting programme at short notice, following the splash of a momentous piece of news. He recalled especially the panel discussion he had arranged to discuss the general implications of the assassination of Sylvanus Olympio in January 1963. History since then had begun to reveal Olympio as essentially the first major victim of a military *coup* in independent Africa. But even then his death appeared in some frightening sense as an omen of things to come. It had been a stunning experience. Julius Nyerere in Tanganyika had wept in public. The first *coup*, the first startling assassination, the first signal of violent decades to follow.

And now the Nigerian Civil War and all its ramified implications compressed in the single poetic tragedy of the death of Christopher Okigbo. What did Hamisi know about this man? What would be the best way of defending him against the charge of subordinating the immortality of art to the transient experience of patriotic fervour?

Abiranja placed his own hand on Hamisi's knee, looked him straight in the eye and said: 'We cannot tell you much more – we cannot give you more advice on how to set about this enterprise. It would be too easy if you were simply to be briefed by your house mates. The whole purpose of the assignment might in fact be to draw you out so that your inner resources in the face of a major assignment can be weighed and assessed. Hamisi, you are on your own!'

It sounded like a solemn sentence in a murder case in the Herebefore. Hamisi swallowed, and turned to look at Salisha. She had tears in her eyes. Then, as if prearranged, both she and Abiranja got up, and left the house silently, yet expressively.

Hamisi sat where he was, his mind numbed. He began gradually to collect himself. Where should he start? He needed to speak to somebody, but whom? He remembered the football match, and then for some reason lines from *The Rime of the Ancient Mariner* came drifting back to him from memories of childhood. Was he remembering or hearing those lines? No, there was a definite difference between this experience and the powerful auditory presence which had spoken the lines from Christopher Okigbo as

they had haunted him since his arrival beyond the horizon
of death.

> Day after day, day after day,
> We stuck, nor breath nor motion;
> As idle as a painted ship
> Upon a painted ocean.
>
> Water, water, everywhere,
> And all the boards did shrink;
> Water, water, everywhere.
> Nor any drop to drink.

Yes, the multitude at the football match came back to him. He
started paraphrasing, 'People, people, everywhere – not a single
ear to listen.' And yet, why not? His first signal for action had at
last come through. He must talk to people, find out the right
people, and see if he could get information relevant to his meta-
historical mission. He must return first to the football stadium.

Hamisi left the house and proceeded to try and find his way
back to the stadium. He could not imagine why there should be
many people still around so long after the soccer match, but he
wanted to sense this presence of multitudes in the hope of winning
a single ear.

He shut the door behind him, and wondered why it was that so
many of the old habits of Herebefore still persisted in the new
Hereafter. Why were doors necessary? Why were street lights
needed? Why indeed was there day and night?

'I suppose the answer lies in the simple proposition that half
the total sum of human happiness consists in the sense of security
afforded by the familiar,' he thought to himself.

So many things in After-Africa were already vastly different
from the state of affairs in Africa of the Herebefore; yet some
underpinnings of familiarity had to be available. The division of
life into days and hours, the years mounting up to centuries, light
and shade, day and night, windows and doors, all these were im-

portant contributions to the theme of continuity which lay between Africa and After-Africa.

Street lights were already on as Hamisi walked back in the direction of the stadium. The crowds had thinned a lot but there were still clusters of agitated analysts of the match in different places along the way. Coffee shops were open, again with cups which though bearing the stamp of a different world nevertheless maintained their unmistakable links with shapes of the Herebefore. Hamisi walked on.

The majesty of the stadium came into view. There were still a few people around near the gates, the charms of analysing the moves of the different players, and the meaning of the monotheistic lead as accomplished in this particular match, were being discussed with great vigour. Hamisi passed by some of these groups, aiming for an exchange with the man who looked like a special watchman at the gates of the stadium.

When he reached him he first made a few comments about the match, of the kind that would not lead to a debate. Then he asked the watchman whether he knew of anybody around who had arrived in After-Africa after being killed in the Nigerian Civil War. The watchman mentioned several names, with their addresses, but none of them seemed to be immediately available. He looked round at the crowds nearby, recognizing perhaps the majority of those involved in agitated conversations in different little clusters. But none of them were victims of the Nigerian Civil War. He was about to direct Hamisi to an address when suddenly his eyes brightened up. 'There is of course Jacob Alobi – he is in the east wing of the stadium right now.'

Hamisi looked at the watchman inquiringly. The watchman said 'Jacob was playing for the Sixteenth Century in this match.'

Hamisi was more puzzled than ever. How could a person killed in the Nigerian Civil War in the second half of the twentieth century be playing on the side of the Sixteenth Century in the soccer match? Perhaps there was a simple explanation, but the main thing was to establish contact with whoever was supposed to know something about the Civil War. The watchman said he would take him to Alobi.

They entered the stadium, the watchman leading and making some comments about the soccer league this year, and the implications for other centuries which lay in the defeat of the Eleventh Century so late in the contest. As they walked towards the east wing of the stadium, Hamisi marvelled afresh at the massive size of the stadium and the intricate complexity of its arrangements to maximize visual effectiveness. The stadium had a number of staircases, some of them escalators, and some of them moving platforms in order to cover the vast distances quickly. The east wing was a little higher than the rest of the stadium, and seemed to have windows more reminiscent of residential buildings than of arenas for sporting contests.

They gradually found their way to the east wing. They took a lift and shot up to the fifth floor. They emerged from the lift, went down the corridors, and stood behind a massive Lamu door, elaborately carved in magnificent neo-Persian patterns. Across the top of the door, rather incongruously and yet also carved, was the message 'Refresher Room'. The watchman gripped the silver knob of the door, turned, and opened. The two people stepped in. The room was dark, at least compared with the outside.

12

It took a minute or two for Hamisi's vision to adjust itself to the dimmer lighting of the Refresher Room. But visual adjustment was to constitute a psychological stumbling-block for, as the contents of the Refresher Room became clear to his vision, the shapes were reduced to a bizarre spectacle. There seemed to be about two dozen naked men, with a similar number of women. Some of the men still wore the beads which had differentiated them on the football ground a few hours ago. The red or white beads, according to whether they were Eleventh or Sixteenth Century, continued to adorn a number of masculine bodies in the room. But in some cases the beads had been removed, and the nakedness of the soccer player had been made complete. There was an air of agitated activity in the group, but on closer observation it became clear that each couple was engaged in one of two possible activities. Either the woman was massaging the man nearest to her, or the man was making love to the woman. These two alternating activities formed an interspersing pattern on the carpeted floor of the Refresher Room.

There was also on closer scrutiny a surprising casualness pervading the atmosphere. In one corner a man was engaged in the regular tempo of primordial communion between the thighs of a woman, and yet somehow continuing a conversation with his neighbour who was having his shoulders massaged. In another corner, a woman was answering a question addressed to her by another woman in the process of parting her legs.

Hamisi stepped back in embarrassment. Was this a guilty orgy or was it natural innocence? Hamisi was profoundly uneasy.

But the watchman, in keeping with the all-pervading casualness of the room, was inquiring from a couple nearest the door where to find Jacob Alobi. A neighbour interrupted his amorous activity, raised himself, and said, 'I think he is near the water fountain. Yes, he is there,' he said, pointing.

The watchman signalled Hamisi and together they found their way to the water fountain, and to a tall naked figure lying on his stomach, enjoying the elegant movements of skilful female fingers massaging the rear side of his ribs.

'Hello, Jacob,' said the watchman. 'I have brought you a chap who is interested in talking to a Nigerian.'

Alobi's physical position did not change, but there was a definite shift in the expression of his eyes. He was obviously interested.

'Sit down,' said Alobi to Hamisi. The watchman took his leave as Hamisi squatted by the side of the long Nigerian body, shimmering in response to intricate hand movements up and down its back.

51

'You are new, aren't you?' Hamisi nodded. 'And I take it you are curious about Nigeria because of the Okigbo case.'

Hamisi nodded, and swallowed in continuing embarrassment. Jacob Alobi noticed, and chuckled. 'You must have come from a more prudish part of Africa!'

Hamisi said where he was from and gave further details about himself. Alobi then said: 'You must remember that sexual privacy in the Herebefore was basically a luxury. One needed to attain a particular standard of living, and be able to afford a particular quality of accommodation, before one could contrive an orgasm behind a curtain of privacy. It is still true to say that at least half the children of Africa who manage to reach the age of seven have at one time or another seen their parents copulating. You must have come from a fairly well-to-do family if you were spared these facts of life!'

Hamisi did not feel any less embarrassed. He felt guilty in addition for being embarrassed.

'Anyhow, what can I tell you about Nigeria?'

It was then that Hamisi explained that he was to be Counsel for Salvation in the Okigbo case. He knew little about Nigeria, or about Christopher Okigbo, or about the system of justice in After-Africa. He needed advice on all these matters, and Alobi was the very first person he was approaching for some briefing.

Hamisi had underestimated how much he did in fact know both about Okigbo and about Nigeria. As Jacob Alobi talked easily, many of the bits of information which came floating in were not entirely unfamiliar to Hamisi. But there were also a number which were new to him. Hamisi was conscious of the fact that he had to make a determined effort to concentrate, particularly as next to Alobi was a couple making love, breathing audibly in gasps of mutual responsiveness. And the impressive body of Alobi himself, delicately manipulated by his woman, was an additional diversion. Yet he managed to listen to tales about Christopher Okigbo's childhood in Ojoto in Eastern Nigeria where he was born in 1932. There was a discussion about his tendency to withdraw into himself at school, his distaste for some of the sports which were organized at school, the mixture of insecurity and arrogance as he cultivated a style of social distance. Then there were the years at Ibadan University with the great excitement of entering new worlds of literature. The classics were an experience: the miracle of Greece, the heritage of Rome, excited the responsiveness of an African adolescent. There remained something cold about Christopher Okigbo, and yet something powerfully individualistic in him. Ibadan drew him out a little more effectively than his previous life had succeeded in doing. He could speak softly, and yet retain liveliness in conversation. His opinions were sometimes a little too strongly formulated, perhaps in deliberate hyperbole. He was the kind of man whose personality depended not on what he looked like but on what he was, complete with his beliefs and the idiosyncracies of his powers of articulation. He would have been disastrous on a public platform – but had a quiet inner power in a conversational duet – a strange mixture of inhibited shyness and almost arrogant self-confidence.

'We did not always understand him when he talked. I certainly didn't understand much of his poetry, though it was quite clear that something clever and deep was coming out of the young man,' continued Alobi.

Hamisi was not quite clear how many of these details he could remember, particularly when Alobi went on to discuss some important Ibo ideas which might have influenced Okigbo's poetry. Idoto was mentioned as a goddess of Okigbo's community in Ijoto, with her shrine beside a sacred river. The oil bean and its intricate sacred symbolism was patiently explained by Alobi. He continued to talk, as he turned round, lying now on his back while the girl massaged his waist. Hamisi tried not to look too closely, particularly as he was aware that Alobi was in full erection. Yet Alobi continued with the details of the old Eastern Nigeria, the verve and ambition of the Ibo, the initial commitment to Pan-Nigerianism combined with the ambition to lead the rest of the population behind energetic Ibo initiative. The striking economic mobility of many of the Ibo as they spread out to other parts of the country and beyond, featured also in Alobi's narrative, partly

53

to illuminate the general context of the riots in the North which were to shatter the faith of the Ibo in the idea of one Nigeria. Christopher Okigbo was one young Ibo among many, well educated and intellectually successful. The old tendency to regard the intellectual achievements of the Ibo as an indication of a communal intellectual gift had not affected Christopher Okigbo quite as deeply as it had distorted the self-evaluation of some of his fellow Ibos. But what Azikiwe had once described as 'the manifest destiny of the Ibo', that feeling of leadership thrust on a gifted tribe, was never entirely absent whenever the Ibo reappraised their place in the nation and in the region as a whole.

Again Hamisi found himself consciously trying to avoid looking into the eyes of Alobi lest he should notice how conscious Hamisi was of Alobi's state of erection.

However Alobi did notice Hamisi's embarrassment. Alobi said, 'Although brought up as a Muslim, you seem to share some of the inhibitions of Christian Africa. In Christian mythology one long-term consequence of the concept of Original Sin was the evolution of the idea of "private parts". Until then these parts of ours were not private. It was the excessive consciousness of their role in sensuality, and the attempt to cover all this up in European and Asiatic civilizations, which gave rise to the aura of secrecy surrounding the parts.'

Hamisi was surprised to learn soon that Alobi could quote Milton with ease on the question of Adam and Eve at a time when their very nakedness was the glory of their innocence.

> *God-like erect, with native honour clad*
> *In naked majesty seemed lords of all,*
> *And worthy seemed, for in their looks divine*
> *The image of their glorious Maker shone . . .*
> *Nor those mysterious parts were then concealed;*
> *Then was not guilty shame; dishonest shame*
> *Of nature's work, honour dishonourable,*
> *Sin-bred, how have ye troubled all mankind*
> *With shows instead, mere shows of seeming pure,*

And banished from man's life his happiest life,
Simplicity and spotless innocence.

Alobi said, 'Obviously this was the time of human evolution when nakedness was not a symbol of sensuous desire, but was a symbol of innocence:

So passed they naked on, nor shunned the sight
Of God or angel, for they thought no ill . . .

Hamisi reflected that much of Africa still retained the primaevalness of the Garden of Eden. It was fitting that the latest archaeological findings put the beginnings of man decisively in East Africa. Hamisi recalled Karamoja region in Uganda. A Karamojong walking around naked on his daily business had in effect divorced his body from sensuality; his nakedness was essentially amoral. But a Westernized African girl in Kampala in a mini-skirt was self-consciously seeking some degree of sexual impact.

Alobi's voice took Hamisi's train of thought a little further, almost as if he knew what he had been thinking about.

'Much of the guilty self-consciousness about sex in Africa came with Christianity; that was what the voluminous *basuti* in Uganda was all about. I understand the *basuti* was partly intended to conceal the female form and promote social discipline by swathing temptation in yards of cloth. The *basuti* was a symbol of Western modesty in the nineteenth century; the mini-skirt is a symbol of Western rebellion against its own modesty. Both symbols were profoundly synthetic.'

Alobi lamented that West Africa had nothing to compare with the Masai and the Karamojong in their primaeval dignity.

'To the Karamojong the very concept of "private parts" was a piece of neo-colonialism. To condemn the organ of procreation to a life of suffocation behind underpants in the tropics was human ingratitude at its worst. It was to condemn a benefactor to the hot experience of strict solitary confinement. A symbol of the continuity of the human race was made a subject of guilt and shame, covered up, and denied direct contact with the great elements of nature in the blazing sun or the torrential tropical rain or the softening caress of an evening breeze.'

But more immediately before his eyes it was a different kind of caress that Hamisi was witnessing. Alobi's naked massage girl was stretching herself across Alobi's body to rub beneath his armpits. As she was leaning across to get to the armpits her breasts were rubbing against Alobi's erect nudity. The rubbing beneath the armpits continued with the hands, pushing the breasts below into brief moments of contact with Alobi's manhood. Hamisi's own pent-up excitement was approaching the boundaries of visual noticeability. But Alobi continued to talk.

13

Alobi had moved from a discussion of nakedness in relation to sex to a discussion of nakedness in relation to poverty. The latter had overwhelmingly to do with the intrusion of dress as a mode of cultural behaviour, and the potentialities of ostentation inherent in dress culture. He was back to a discussion of the Nigerian Civil War and the kind of nakedness to which many were sentenced in the wake of great deprivation. The Western conscience had been alerted by pictures of naked children in Biafra; but the hungry nudity of their parents behind the scene had deeper themes of pathos. If sacrifice was a measure of greatness, then some Ibo were born great, some became great, but many others had greatness thrust upon them. Many a married couple made love in order to forget that they were hungry.

The war had dragged on, relentlessly, pitilessly. 'Some of us forgot what life was like without fresh memories of someone just deceased.'

Hamisi remembered that Alobi had never mentioned how he himself had met his end. He asked him now precisely this.

Alobi answered, 'You should surely know by now that it was

not an *end* in any case!' He laughed aloud at his own joke and turned a little to give his massage girl greater scope with his left side.

Alobi continued: 'Actually I died in an air crash. Don't you remember R. E. G. Armattoe's poem *The Way I Would Like to Die?*'

> *This is the way I'd like to go,*
> *If you must know.*
> *I would like to go while still young,*
> *While the dew is wet on the grass;*
> *To perish in a great air crash,*
> *With a silver 'plane burning bright*
> *Like a flashing star in the night;*
> *While the huge wreckage all ablaze,*
> *Shines brightly for my last embrace,*
> *I'd like to see the flames consume*
> *Each nerve and bone and hair and nail,*
> *Till of dust naught but ash remains.*
> *Or as stone, swiftly sink unseen.*
> *But if I should hear someone wail,*
> *Because dust has gone back to dust,*
> *Mad with fury, I shall return*
> *To smite the poor wretch on the head.*
> *So, let me go when I am young,*
> *And the dew is still on the fern,*
> *With a silver 'plane burning bright,*
> *Like a flashing star in the night.*

Alobi commented, 'Raphael Armattoe was forty when he died, wasn't he? In 1953 he had led a delegation to the United Nations to rally support for the idea of a union of French and British Togo. On his way back he died in an accident in Germany, but it was not an air crash. He left it to me to die in an air crash fifteen years later.'

Alobi explained that he had assignments to negotiate for arms' supplies among various dealers. In Lisbon he dealt with both Portuguese dealers and South African dealers, and for his money he preferred South Africans. They were in many ways more efficient and reliable, and in a strange way more loyal to the Biafran cause, than the Portuguese could ever claim to be. Alobi had also been to Paris three times on missions connected with arms' supplies, but in fact the supplies came from outside France very often. Europe was still full of friends, but even more it was full of astute businessmen. But who could blame Biafra? A sovereign government already recognized had enormous advantages in relation to accepted prejudices of orthodox diplomacy. The Federal Government of Nigeria had a whole year of undisputed legitimacy in the capitals of most of the countries of the world before adequate voices were raised in defence of the rights of Biafra.

Alobi's last day in Africa was a Wednesday. 'It's funny how many societies in Africa opt to include among the names they give to their newly born the name of the day on which they are born. The most famous Saturday in the history of contemporary Africa is the Saturday of *Kwame* Nkrumah. It might have been a good idea if, on entering After-Africa, we assumed the name of the day on which we died. It might be worth raising this question at the next meeting of the Assembly of the Ages.'

Hamisi remembered hearing that the Assembly of the Ages was the great legislative body which received suggestions from different members of After-Africa and passed legislation to govern certain aspects of life beyond the grave. Hamisi again reflected how vastly more democratic life beyond the grave was than most religions in the Herebefore had implied. The massive authoritarianism of God sitting in judgement, which had been assumed by both Christians and Muslims, as indeed by members of other faiths, seemed in retrospect to have been a figment of barren earthly imagination. The Assembly of the Ages had wide areas of latitude independent of the Almighty.

Alobi proceeded to talk about the day he died. It was extraordinary that even under the impact of such recollections, with all the terror and sorrow they might have recaptured, Alobi's manhood remained defiantly erect. It was as if this part of his body acted independently of the moods of his mind. But Hamisi was at a stage when the girl's body was even more disconcerting although it betrayed no signs of sexual responsiveness. Hamisi observed the sensuous torso, the curvature of the breasts from the side, the dark skin glistening in its own soft perspiration against the subdued light of the Refresher Room.

' "I am losing height!" cried the pilot.' Alobi was narrating. 'We were flying at night to protect the good name of the religious organization. The deal in Gabon had been successfully carried out, and when we checked the plane before departure it seemed to be in better shape than some of the machines we had had to use on occasion. Yoanna, the Israeli pilot, had demonstrated his craftsmanship in no uncertain terms. We left for Enugu full of optimism, happy with the conclusion of our mission, and in high spirits.

'But then the Fokker Friendship began to lose height. Had an engine failed? Had we overloaded the vehicle? Had there been a fuel leakage?

'In a desperate move, born more out of puzzlement than of scientific diagnosis, Yoanna ordered that we push out some of the equipment. Even the very exercise of pushing it out nearly forced the plane to somersault its way to a grand explosion. But we accomplished this mission, and the plane seemed to level out, and then began to ascend. All too briefly, we thought the problem was solved. We had negotiated hard for the equipment for the war, and were now throwing it down in a bid to save ourselves. Weapons of death thrown down the firmament in exchange for the promise of survival.

'And yet it did not work.' Alobi had caught sight of Father Rambino making the sign of the cross. In a bizarre reflection Alobi had wondered if the shape of the plane was not itself enough of a cross. He had turned to look at Yoanna in the pilot's cockpit, observed the relentless experimentation with the different switches and gears, the anxious reading of those multiple clocks of eternity. And then the creeping shiver – a dawning realization

59

that death was beckoning the plane downwards. Alobi's body had stiffened, and he knew he was afraid. He could see the darkness, and the deeper darkness of the clouds, punctuated by glimmerings of taunting stars. He thought of friends who had died before him and tried to convert the prospect of seeing them again into a moment of solace as the sense of doom crowded in on them.

' "We may be able to do a crash landing," said Yoanna. "I think this part of the country is relatively flat. There is a chance." '

Alobi recounted 'We almost believed him. We so desperately needed to believe him. But then we saw that the night outside was no longer quite as dark. With terrifying clarity the wing of the plane commanded our attention. It had assumed a bright majesty of sheer fire, scorching the clouds which drifted by.'

> *The stars have departed,*
> *the sky in monocle*
> *surveys the worldunder.*
>
> *The stars have departed,*
> *and I – where am I?*

Alobi saw the priest reach for his throat and start coughing. He saw Yoanna turn backwards to look at them, a look of simple but devastating despair.

'The plane got hotter. I saw the growing flames through the window and wondered what we looked like from below – perhaps a meteorite in the splendour of descent, perhaps a ball of fire burning its way through the firmament. I suppose I thought big in order to boost up my courage. The priest was kneeling, praying, and sobbing. A certain rage engulfed me, quite irrationally. I reached for the man, caught him by the collar, and shouted "Shut up!" It was the last thing I remember. I am still not sure whether we crashed soon after, or whether I simply lost my memory as my body sizzled in that compact hell floating in the African sky.'

60

Alobi was silent for a minute. Even his massage girl stopped massaging. The position of his manhood had not changed, yet his inner attention was riveted to a single incident of a vastly different experience. Then he smiled as he said, 'We gate-crashed our way into this new world. It was a magnificent exit out of the old one.'

Alobi, Hamisi, and the girl again stayed still. And in that stillness Hamisi once again began to sense the girl's presence. This time he saw her full face for the first time. There was a proud gentleness about it. The eyelashes were not particularly long, and yet there was a spacing out which commanded lingering attention. The chin was perhaps a little too sharp, and yet if the eyes were looking simultaneously at the chin and the mouth there was a relationship of proportion more easily discerned than described. The nose was small, somewhat flattened out at the base, but again bearing a relationship of proportion when the cheeks were simultaneously in view. The girl's eyes looked at Hamisi for the first time. She then looked at Alobi inquiringly. Alobi suddenly sat up, and turned to Hamisi saying, 'I am so sorry but would you like a massage too?'

Hamisi swallowed hard. He looked at the girl again down her neck, past her shoulders, and further below. Alobi explained that the girls were made available to the soccer players. Those who had won received the attention of the girls as a reward for their victory. Those who had lost received that attention as a consolation for their defeat. That was why both teams were in that room together, being refreshed after two hours of contest and several weeks of practice. The prize for the victors and the consolation for the vanquished were the delicate skills of entertainment afforded by the girls of the Refresher Room of that majestic stadium.

But African socialism was nothing if it was not an exercise in *ad hoc* hospitality. Since Hamisi had come visiting Alobi in the Refresher Room, the girl would be happy to extend to him the services she was rendering Alobi.

Hamisi continued to look at her, swallowed hard, tensed up

61

towards a decision – but remembered that he had a week in which to prepare his brief in defence of Christopher Okigbo. He thanked the girl and Alobi with an embarrassed stammer. He asked Alobi for advice about whom else he should see. Then he rose, and staggered towards the exit. As he was going out he looked back. It was the girl now who was lying on her back and Alobi was in readiness. Hamisi cleared his throat and shut the door behind him.

14

It was a staggering sight. The trial of Christopher Okigbo was opening at the Grand Stadium. They came in their millions. The multitude in white were strikingly reminiscent of the great processions of Muslim pilgrims pouring forth from Mount Arafat to return to the Kaaba in Mecca. The Grand Stadium of After-Africa was assuming today the sacred stature of the Kaaba, multiplied a hundred times in size and a thousand times in visual impact. They were marching towards the Grand Stadium, drawn from every geographical corner, every historical time associated with Africa's place in eternity. The men came, the women came, and the children followed by the side of their parents.

The varying features of Africa's humanity through the ages were fully represented. The short, the tall and the stout edged their way towards Okigbo's trial. Thick lips and thin, flat noses and straight, the full richness of Africa's heritage of hair, the full diversity of Africa's legacy of colours.

Individuals once famous in the Herebefore could be spotted among the crowds. Yes, there again was Chaka, the Zulu, fat, still sensuously exuberant, the scar against his forehead noticeable from a distance, the cruel turn of his upper lip lending mysterious dignity to what would otherwise have been a rather foolish and rounded face. Chaka was engaged in an animated discussion as he walked towards the Grand Stadium. The companion by his side was Mirambo, the hero of Nyamwezi around Lake Nyasa and Lake Tanganyika. This Ngoni hero had a lot in common with the Zulu warrior. The weapons which had been used in the Nigerian Civil War were so vastly different from what they had had to employ in their own wars in Africa. Chaka and Mirambo both believed that much of the heroism of war had in any case been diluted by the massive impersonality of advanced technology. Mirambo in a famous debate had even once put forward a political philosophy of what he called 'military liberalism'. By this he meant a kind of warfare which called forth from the individual warrior his own internal resources, testing his courage in hand-to-hand combat, allowed him autonomy of initiative and individual skill, and subjected him only to minimal organization within a broad military strategy. The kind of warfare which Mirambo and Chaka had led permitted within a dictatorial structure a high degree of military individualism. But modern technology had destroyed the ethic of individualism, not only in politics but also in war. Man had become increasingly incidental. The masses were the new yardstick for great decisions – how to mobilize the masses, how to serve the masses, how to destroy the masses. A spectator from a distance looking at Chaka and Mirambo in lively conversation could safely bet that they were discussing disparagingly the kind of war which Nigerians and Biafrans had been waging – all those fighter planes flown by Egyptians or Portuguese; all those hand grenades, rockets, and machine-guns. Where were the spear and the shield of honour? Where were the symbols of African manliness? Africa was learning faster how to destroy the masses militarily than she was learning how to mobilize them politically. Chaka nodded vigorous agreement with the well-known views of Mirambo as they approached the gates of the Grand Stadium.

The bearded man coming down the hill, wasn't that Barghash, the old Sultan of Zanzibar? A century separated him from Patrice Lumumba, and yet they too were engaged in vigorous discussion, presumably connected with the trial that they were about to attend.

A figure who attracted particular notice was Sir Abubakar Tafawa Balewa, the first Prime Minister of independent Nigeria. People pointed him out to each other as they found their way to the Grand Stadium. Would the trial be a trial of Balewa and his regime? Was Balewa a victim of Nigeria's instability? Or was he one of its many causes? It all depended upon the turn which the trial would take. The issues were big, and a figure of Tafawa's stature in the first few years of Nigeria's independence could hardly fail to be touched by the scorching issues which burst forth out of the bubbling nationhood of Nigeria.

Within the stadium Salisha had obtained a strategic seat as she watched that vast receptacle absorb all those human millions. The stadium had looked full for the football match, and yet that was a misleading indication of its capacity. Today's millions were a test of the stadium's infinite elasticity.

The grass of the football field was still there, but in the middle of it all a huge stage had been erected, designed to be the great arena for a mighty battle of judicial wit. On one side of the shining wooden stage in the middle of the soccer ground was an enclosure of nine seats. These were the seats of the nine Elders who would be listening to the arguments advanced by the two Counsels in the case. The nine seats were themselves like thrones carved out of ebony, the back-rests being rounded with red-covered cushioning in the middle, with a thin ivory frame. The arm-rests were cushioned too, but curiously enough with antelope skin on top. The cumulative visual effect of nine red cushions and eighteen antelope arm-rests on the spectators in the stadium was bizarre but impressive. In some strange way it was like looking at the hides of nine bulls freshly killed in the stadium at Madrid, neatly arranged across the arena in patterns of relationship with nine red flags of the matador next to the bleeding hides.

The nine Elders were not as yet in attendance. Neither were the Counsels. The crowds were still coming in, but the hour of commencement was at hand.

As the last of the multitudes were finding their way to their seats a sign as old as creation in the universe burst upon the multitude. It was the signal of thunder – clear, penetrating, a thousand times more gripping than the loudest explosions of the sky on the shores of Victoria Nyanza.

It was one thunderous shake. But everyone seemed to know its meaning. There, in numbers beyond the imagination of census collectors, one suddenly saw a whole universe of humanity rise in unison to attention. As far as the eye could see in that stadium, white-robed figures stood in attentive response as the skies of After-Africa announced the entry of the nine Elders of Judgement. They too were partly in white, but their white garments were *agbadas* rather than *kanzus*, bound round the edges with thick red and gold borders. The simple addition of these borders to those white garments sharply differentiated the judges from the multitude. All the nine Elders had beards of varying sizes, two were bald, four had gone grey very conspicuously. They moved towards their thrones in strides pregnant with purpose, yet unhurried in their deliberation. The rest of the stadium stood in silent attention watching aged wisdom on parade.

On reaching their thrones the nine Elders sat down. The rest of the stadium continued to stand. There was a moment of expectancy. And then all eyes turned towards the South Gate to witness the entry of Counsel for Damnation, Kwame Apolo-Gyamfi, in a flowing white Ghanaian toga, edged with green. The crowd held its breath. Young Apolo-Gyamfi was one of the most brilliant Africans produced by the twentieth century. He was himself nearly committed for trial when he entered After-Africa in the 1940s after an act of tragic impatience at Oxford. But instead of a trial he was conceded more than two decades of uncertainty before being given a test. Many had wondered since the 1940s what kind of test would be given to young Kwame Apolo-Gyamfi when the moment came. But it now seemed clear that his test too was to be connected with the trial of Christopher Okigbo. Counsel for Damnation, he was, in the language of the Herebefore, the voice of the State against Christopher Okigbo. He halted at the South Gate, standing to attention, short in stature and yet with an intellectual reputation which gave him an immense presence in that immense context.

A second later his judicial antagonist, Hamisi Salim, appeared opposite him at the North Gate. The two gates were at the edges of the football field, the trial stage was in the middle, the Judges were already presiding. Hamisi was much taller than Apolo-Gyamfi. In sheer physical impact Hamisi should have commanded more immediate attention, standing six foot one inch, clothed in a shimmering *juba* in *lasi*, with an elaborately patterned grey shawl of the kind imported into Mombasa for centuries from the craftsmen of the Persian Gulf.

The two young people looked at each other for the first time. Of the two, Hamisi was easily the more nervous, and this was observable even from the furthest seat of that infinite colosseum. It may have been because he was newer to After-Africa than his opponent, or it may have been because he had greater humility. A touch of intellectual arrogance had been a major trait of Apolo-Gyamfi in the Herebefore, though life beyond the grave had blunted some of the edges of that arrogance. On balance, at least according to the prejudices of the Herebefore, Apolo-Gyamfi was a less likeable person than Hamisi Salim, and yet that was too easy a judgement. The kind of pride which animated Apolo-Gyamfi included within itself moral resources, in spite of the fact that it had also been pride which had led him to a hasty miscalculation at Oxford. The two men stood and waited, the multitudes stood and waited, and the nine Elders of Judgement presided in silence. And then the skies parted once again to announce in ringing terms the next phase of the proceedings.

The two Counsels stepped forth from the gates, approached each other, stood facing each other, and then turned together shoulder to shoulder to face in the direction of the Elders. They then marched in eloquent purposefulness towards the grand stage. There were a few steps from the grass upwards on to the platform. They climbed those steps, almost in unison. The crowd watched. Silence continued to reign.

The two men, acquiring a strange complementarity despite the

66

contrast of their physical heights, stood shoulder to shoulder a second longer and then knelt simultaneously. Another thunderous signal shattered the silence. The trial had begun.

15

Apolo-Gyamfi was on his feet, presenting the case for Damnation. The Elders of Judgement sat on their thrones, in a mood of relaxed concentration. Hamisi Salim sat in a chair on the north corner of the raised platform, at once nervous and intensely attentive. The Grand Stadium was listening.

Where was Christopher Okigbo, the accused? Hamisi had learnt by this time that in After-Africa it was considered barbaric to have the accused standing in the dock, conspicuously displayed in isolation, silent while others talked about him in his presence, subject to glares of spectators, denied the right of private anguish while his fate was being decided.

But did not the accused also have the right to know what went on in the great dialogue preceding a decision on his fate? The rules of judicial practice in After-Africa gave the accused the right to see everything that went on at the trial. He could choose between attending the proceedings as a spectator among the millions who filled this stadium, or he could remain in his own room, looking at one specified blank wall which, with concentration, he could convert into something comparable to a large television screen of the Herebefore. Hamisi was not sure whether Christopher Okigbo was in the audience among those millions in white, or was watching and listening to his own trial in private anguish at home.

Apolo-Gyamfi was describing what he called 'the fall of Okigbo'. Counsel made a distinction between individualism, universalism, and social collectivism. A great artist was first of all an individualist, secondly a universalist, and only thirdly a social collectivist. Individualism was the deeper loyalty to one's inner

67

being, a capacity to retain a private area of distinctiveness in one's personality. The right to be eccentric was one great unit of measurement. The black sheep of the family was the greatest individualist member, precisely by being the most conspicuously distinctive.

Apolo-Gyamfi continued: 'Universalism, on the other hand, is a commitment to the eternal. The frontiers of space and the boundaries of time relinquish their legitimacy. A fusion of the near and the distant, of the now and the ever, is what universalism is all about.'

As for social collectivism, Apolo-Gyamfi defined it as that complex of loyalties which tied the individual to his own specific society, which commanded his affections for his kith and kin, which aroused his protectiveness for the soil of his ancestors, which enabled him to serve and, very occasionally, to love his people. Socialism, tribalism, and nationalism, were all different forms of these bonds of collectivity.

'We in After-Africa have gone beyond the naïve egalitarianism which ignored the great differentials in nature's endowment. It is simply untrue to regard the death of Christopher Okigbo as being no more significant than that of an upright but simple fellow tribesman. All life is sacred, but some lives are more sacred than others.'

Counsel then went on to claim that the duty of a very gifted person is fundamentally different from the duty of a more ordinary being. It may well be true that the common man's first duty is a duty to his own society, to the precise collectivity which produced him and nourished him into communal consciousness. The ordinary man is permitted to be first and foremost a social collectivist. He need never experience the depths of individualism, nor need he be called upon to bow to the dictates of the universal.

'But it is different with the gifted. Small men have duties only to their societies; great men have duties to mankind.'

Apolo-Gyamfi proceeded to categorize different types of intellectual greatness, and the ethical duties which were born out of them. He discussed C. P. Snow's analysis of the two cultures – of science and the arts, but drew attention to the ethical poverty of Snow's conclusions.

'If we are now to regrade the obligations of the artist as against the scientist, we must surely observe one important difference. The duty of the scientist is, firstly, to the universal; secondly, to the social; and only thirdly to himself. But the duty of the artist is firstly to himself, secondly to the universal, and only thirdly to the social. The inner creativity of the artist requires a doctrine of the primacy of the self. The aesthetic meaning of the artist requires a supporting doctrine of aesthetic universalism. But it is by serving the universal that the artist should be expected to serve his own society.'

Apolo-Gyamfi asserted that the life of Christopher Okigbo became a distortion of these values. From childhood to artistic adulthood, Christopher Okigbo was the supreme individual. He seemed to dislike great crowds, and certainly disliked the idea of addressing great crowds, even in poetic terms. His individualism sometimes had a ring of intellectual arrogance, or was it simply aristocratic distance? It was Okigbo who once remarked to delegates at a conference, 'I don't read my poems to non-poets!'.

The very occasion on which he said this was rare in its collectiveness. It was at a conference held at Makerere University College in Kampala in 1962. At that conference, Okigbo gave one of his rare public talks, condescending to collectivize literary explanation.

In some ways it was just as well that he did not permit himself too much exposure to public 'culturalization'. He was not a platform performer. His high-pitched voice was somewhat distracting when raised to be heard by a crowd. His somewhat eccentric mannerisms also diluted his potential for impact. But the voice of his poetry made up for any shortcomings of his own.

In Okigbo, until the explosion of Ibo separatism, individualism and universalism were beautifully intertwined. He used to deny that he was an African poet. 'I am a poet', was his simple insistence. In 1964, he had become even more explicit. 'There is no

African literature. There is good writing and bad writing – that's all.'

Then came the great Festival of Negro Art in Dakar in 1966. It was a great cultural occasion for black people, and an excuse for some brilliant if synthetic devices of 'culturalization'. There was also real art, deep in its meaning, hungry in its passion, alive in compulsive communication.

Who was Africa's greatest poet for the Festival? Christopher Okigbo was offered the First Prize for poetry. A sense of admiration pervaded the climate of judgement. Some other poets swallowed hard, proudly accepting that extra margin of greatness in Okigbo's lines. A few poets were more sceptical, less convinced of the aesthetic accuracy of the verdict. Some of the latter might also in turn have been envious.

But a startling pronouncement was made. Chris Okigbo had rejected the First Prize for poetry awarded by the Festival of Negro Arts. Why? His answer had once again that aggressive fanaticism of the paramount universalist. He had proclaimed, 'There is no such thing as Negro art.'

Apolo-Gyamfi, turning to the Elders in the Grand Stadium of After-Africa, said, 'Oh, wise Elders of Judgement, consider the point of departure of this great young man. When he refused the prize which fellow black people were awarding him, sharing in the pride of his achievement, he was refusing to mix art with nationalism. However, this same young man who had proclaimed the universality of what is valuable, later put in a uniform, helped himself to a gun, and engaged in a fratricidal war. At the Festival of Negro Art in Dakar Okigbo had refused to dilute art with the milk of nationalism. On the desolate battlefields of Biafra he was to dilute art with the blood of tribalism.'

Apolo-Gyamfi paused, permitting his argument to achieve its optimum effect. The great Elders pondered over the train of Apolo-Gyamfi's reasoning, impressed both by its intellectual vigour and by the moral fervour which characterized the delivery. The concluding epigram of the dilution of art had been effectively utilized. There was a slight release of tension among the multitudes in the stadium, people exchanged comments on the case as so far presented, feet were shifted.

Apolo-Gyamfi then proceeded to discuss the great influences on Okigbo's poetry. Okigbo himself had acknowledged his debt to a variety of literatures and cultures, from classical times to the present day, in English, Latin, Greek, 'a little French, a little Spanish'.

To use Okigbo's own words, 'If those sources have become assimilated into an integral whole it is difficult to sort them out – to know where the Babylonian influence ends and the Classical starts.' The sentence itself captured the theme of continuity in art, of fusion in civilized values, and of eternity as a creative process.

Yet this great man who had once recognized the grand panorama of human experience, dwindled into a petty negotiator for the merchandise of violence. He descended from the mountain of human vision into the swamp of tribal warfare.

Hamisi, listening, remembered Jacob Alobi's account of the plane crash which killed him. But, arising out of his further investigations, Hamisi also recalled another plane load of arms which had crashed in the Cameroons. Christopher Okigbo's personal effects were discovered in the wreckage. Had he died in that crash? If so, where was his body? It had later turned out that Okigbo was alive, and in Birmingham after all. He had indeed been engaged in negotiations which led to the purchase of the arms and their shipment to Eastern Nigeria. That was before the outbreak of the war, but after the tightening up of tensions between the East and the Federal Government. The East was in preparation for a ghastly exercise. Okigbo was to have flown with the arms, but at the last minute he decided to let the merchandise go on its own. He was spared – in order to die another day.

Apolo-Gyamfi was saying, 'These are the charges that we are levelling against Chris Okigbo, Elders of Judgement. A gift of nature was squandered on a battlefield. An imagination which would normally have had another three decades of creativity was offered as a sacrifice. Art is a compact between those who are

71

living, those who are dead, and those who are to be born. Art owes to the ancestors the nourishment of prior achievement, the cumulative influence of past ages. Art owes to its contemporaries the great experience of immediate revelation, the opportunity of being the first critic of what could be imperishable, the chance to watch a piece of eternity emerge from a womb. Art owes to future generations a connecting link between the cumulative accomplishments of the past and the emerging potential of the future.

'If the great artist has to sacrifice himself for anything, he should only sacrifice himself for the universal. To die for the truth is martyrdom. To die for knowledge is martyrdom. To die for art is martyrdom. But when a great thinker or a great artist dies for his nation, that is an indulgence. He has put the politics of the nation before the power of the eternal. He may not have broken his contract with those already dead, but he has broken his contract with the living and with those who are to be born.'

Apolo-Gyamfi concluded with the words: 'When the ordinary man or the great soldier dies for his nation that is indeed heroism. When the great thinker or the great creator dies for his nation that is escapism. Elders of the Ages and of Judgement, that is our case against Christopher Okigbo, newly deceased from Biafra.'

16

The Grand Stadium had again been reduced to meditative silence as Apolo-Gyamfi resumed his seat. It had been a brilliant performance as far as it went. Many regarded it the best opening statement by a Counsel for Damnation for five hundred years or more.

There were a number of people in the audience who knew in detail Apolo-Gyamfi's background, and the circumstances of his arrival in After-Africa. He was born into a well-to-do legal family in Kumasi early in the 1920s. He was sent to Achimota in Accra and soon established himself as both a brilliant debater and a versatile student. He became famous prematurely, partly through his winning a West African essay competition, promoted by the Imperial Literature Bureau in London, and widely contested throughout English-speaking West Africa. Kwame Apolo-Gyamfi had in fact been one of the youngest participants in the competition. The competition was open to school children between the ages of fourteen and nineteen. No one knew for certain why these particular ages were chosen, but they did allow for a wide area of competition. A large number of contestants could not give the precise dates on which they were born. It was permissible for them to estimate their ages, and get their father, or some other elder relative, to confirm that the estimate was not too far out. It is conceivable that many young people over the age of nineteen were in fact admitted into the competition, though it was unlikely that any below the age of fourteen joined the intellectual scramble.

Kwame Apolo-Gyamfi was only just fourteen when he entered the field. The choice of subjects in the essay competition was unrestricted. By an incredible prophetic accident, Apolo-Gyamfi chose to write on the subject of 'The Concept of Judgement in Law and Art'. The very choice of subject was remarkable for a child of fourteen. Its handling by the young boy was a startling experience for those who evaluated the manuscript in London. A discreet commissioner was sent out to the Gold Coast, to verify the authenticity and originality of Apolo-Gyamfi's contribution. The commissioner tactfully discussed the problem with the head of Achimota and teachers were brought in to give confidential evidence about Apolo-Gyamfi's intellectual calibre and level of honesty. Finally the commissioner asked to see young Kwame Apolo-Gyamfi. He discussed with him closely some of the major points raised in the essay. There was no question that the young man, whether inspired externally or not, had completely assimilated the material he had handled in that essay.

The award went to this young genius. A special note of distinction was proclaimed. The newspapers in the Gold Coast, Nigeria, Sierra Leone, and Liberia took up the story with tremen-

73

dous gusto. Apolo-Gyamfi was lionized. He became an intellectual hero a little before his time. This premature fame may have contributed to the tragedy which awaited him at Oxford.

But if anyone was musing about Apolo-Gyamfi's background, his train of recollection was interrupted. The signal of the elements thundered out again across the skies, commanding attention and decreeing the next stage of the trial.

It was now the turn of Counsel for Salvation to make his opening statement. Hamisi Salim rose, tall and resplendent in his *juba*, but his nervousness was apparent to everyone. To be cast in a battle of argument with Kwame Apolo-Gyamfi was a severe test. He had the further handicap of having had a shorter period in After-Africa than his legal antagonist on that stage.

But Hamisi had thought out his case carefully, hoping to strengthen it by the kind of witnesses he would call. He had learnt that the witnesses need not be from Nigeria, or even people who knew very much about the issues underlying the Civil War. Witnesses who were to turn up in person had to be already dead. But they need not be from After-Africa – they could come or be summoned from After-Asia, or even After-Europe. But the great stumbling-block was that neither Counsel was permitted to discuss with the witness in advance the evidence which was to be brought out. It was one of the skills of this kind of trial that Counsels should choose witnesses by objective calculation of their likely utility. Counsels were expected in the course of the proceedings themselves to bring out the evidence of the witnesses in a manner best calculated to serve their own side of the case. It was considered to be bad form to attempt a prior briefing of a witness, even indirectly. It had therefore become conventionally bad form even to consult with a witness before the event.

Counsel had right of access to as much information about the witness as was available in the Bureau of Information among the offices located on the east wing of the Grand Stadium. Substantial biographical data of every person who has ever lived or died was available at the Bureau of Information. It was up to each Counsel to go into the catalogue, assessing likely witnesses, and then prepare their pattern of questions in the hope of drawing out their witnesses to the maximum benefit of their own side.

But could Counsel invite evidence from people still in the Here-before? The great Assembly of the Ages had once discussed the possibility of transporting living people on earth in their sleep and bringing out their subconscious to the world beyond the grave in order to give evidence before important trials. The issue had been hotly debated. There had in fact been a precedent of this kind of transporation in the ascent of the Prophet Muhammad on the night of the Miraj. While sleeping in Mecca, the Prophet had in a single night been transported to Jerusalem, and then upwards to Heaven to participate in a case which decided how many times each day the believers were to be called upon to pray. Muhammad had defended his followers against the excessive demands made by his Maker. Five prayers a day was the great compromise, the mitigated sentence which God passed on humanity. The original sentence before the Miraj was ten times that number.

But could the same principle of summoning the living to come into the world beyond the grave and commune with the dead and with God now be invoked as a method of subpoena? The Assembly of the Ages, after four and a half decades of debate, decided against summoning the living in their sleep to come and give testimony against the dead. The liberal caucus in the Assembly of the Ages had won. One of their arguments had been that such an invasion of the subconscious of the living for such a purpose was a flagrant violation of the privacy of the mind.

But a compromise formula had at last been accepted by the Assembly of the Ages. In a trial in After-Africa the voices of the living could be summoned as witnesses provided what those voices uttered were genuine thoughts which had passed through the minds of the living. It was thus possible for Counsel in a trial to call into evidence even a momentary thought which had once crossed the mind of someone living on earth. In some sense this was also a kind of invasion of the privacy of the minds of the living, but it was not as flagrant as what had originally been proposed when the issue of summoning the living to testify against the dead was first introduced as a proposal in the Assembly of the Ages.

General Gowon of the Federal side and Colonel Ojukwu of Biafra were still alive in the Herebefore. They could not be summoned to give testimony before the Elders of Judgement in this trial of Christopher Okigbo. But their utterances on earth, and even the thoughts that might have crossed their minds relevant to this case, could be summoned before the Elders. The very voices of Ojukwu or Gowon would then be heard in that Grand Stadium, articulating those of their own thoughts which had never before been expressed in audible words or rearticulating statements they had themselves previously made on earth.

But would Counsel be calling for the voices of the actual leaders in the Nigerian Civil War? In some ways this would be too obvious, and part of the skill of trials of this kind was to discover profound links that might otherwise escape notice, rather than simply to go for the obvious witnesses in a case. Nevertheless a lot depended on what Counsel made of the witnesses that he summoned, be those witnesses Nigerian or non-Nigerian, from After-Africa or from without, from the ranks of the dead or from the voices of the living.

Hamisi began his opening statement. He congratulated Kwame Apolo-Gyamfi on a brilliant presentation. He only wished destiny had been as kind to him as it had been to Apolo-Gyamfi. He, Hamisi, had not been briefed by good fortune to start thinking about judgement in art and in law from the age of fourteen. He must therefore apologize if his eloquence should sound less polished, less rehearsed, than the eloquence of honourable Kwame Apolo-Gyamfi.

There was a stir in the Stadium. A good fight was enjoyed in After-Africa perhaps with greater relish than it had ever been enjoyed elsewhere. The soccer matches commanded so much attention partly because, at their best, they were skilful contests with swift movements. A great trial like that of Chris Okigbo at the Grand Stadium was in some ways much more than a football match: it afforded moments of moral revaluation seldom attained even in the great balancing act for the maintenance of a 'mono-theistic lead' which a soccer game sometimes became. And yet the element of a battle of wits, exploration of weakness, skilful manipulation of advantage, linked the experience of an intellectual debate to the experience of a soccer match adroitly executed.

Hamisi proceeded to discuss Kwame Apolo-Gyamfi's three categories: individualism, universalism, and social collectivism. Hamisi asserted that Apolo-Gyamfi's tripartite distinction was excessively European. The idea that great creativity derives from individualism was itself not universally true. Much of Africa's art was a collective experience. The legends, the folk songs, the folk tales, the proverbs, the trance of the primaeval dance, were all shared moments of being.

Much of the poetry was intended to be sung. It was not just the private eye of the reader which was called upon to appreciate poetry; it was more the public ear of the listener. Great art in Europe may have been at best a mode of communication; great art in Africa had always been a flow of interaction. Apolo-Gyamfi's description of the artist as being ultimately a person loyal to himself as an individual must therefore be dismissed as an alien idio-syncracy imported from the principles of European aesthetics and wrongly invoked to pass judgement on a great African artist.

Salisha, sitting a hundred-and-seventy-three rows upwards in the Stadium, swallowed hard with a sense of pride. She reflected with amusement that Hamisi was wrong in his assertion that destiny had not prepared him for this role. He may not have won an essay competition on the concept of judgement in art and in law, but journalism in its day-to-day quest for the meaning of events could also be a good preparation in this respect: those panel discussions on the B.B.C. which Hamisi had moderated or otherwise participated in, those hurriedly prepared talks feverishly interpreting the events of the day for the radio listener thousands of miles away, those quick readings of books so that they could be reviewed and evaluated, those dialogues with transient participants in Hamisi's radio programmes. Salisha's eyes moistened as she recalled one dialogue, prophetic in also having been concerned with Christopher Okigbo. She recalled the events of that night in London, the polished conversation she had had with Hamisi, the invitation to his flat, his skilful preparation for a moment of masculine conquest, and her ultimate philosophical surrender. Now there he was, dear Hamisi, a little less nervous than at the beginning, proving almost equal to the dazzling brilliance of Kwame Apolo-Gyamfi.

The Elders of Judgement sat on their thrones listening with that inscrutable air of private concentration. Apolo-Gyamfi sat in his corner, a little man with a massive presence, also deeply attentive. He was interested in more than what Hamisi was saying. He had become interested in Hamisi.

17

Counsel for Salvation was still on his feet. He had analysed some of Okigbo's poetry in terms of its demands on the public ear of the listener. It was true that much of Okigbo's poetry owed something to a cultural heritage external to Africa. It had also been suggested by some critics that the obscurity of Okigbo's lines was a case of subordinating meaning to imagery. Traditional African poetry had to be understood if it was to be a collective experience. There had to be a meaning to what was being formulated in poetic terms. Evocative pictures in words could be a case of brilliant imagery, but not an adequate instance of meaningful interaction.

And yet these critics forgot that Okigbo's poetry did not consist merely in evocative visual images, but also in the power of sound and the excitement of listening. By paying special attention to the music of poetry, Okigbo had been loyal to the tradition of song in Africa's aesthetic experience. The poem in the village had been sung partly because it had also to be an adventure in aesthetic listening. In a language alien to Africa, and sometimes in expressions borrowed from elsewhere, Okigbo had nevertheless been loyal to the primordial fusion of word with sound, of image with music, or simply of song. And then, willed almost unconsciously by Hamisi, a voice from the sky suddenly filled the Grand Stadium. There was a resonant and vibrant articulation which arrested the attention of that vast multitude as three short lines from the poetry of Christopher Okigbo momentarily filled the universe.

> *Then we must sing, tongue-tied,*
> *Without name or audience,*
> *Making harmony among the branches.*

Silence followed, a point had been made, the Elders, the crowds, Salisha, and Counsel for Damnation waited for Hamisi to continue.

Hamisi moistened his lips with his tongue, cleared his throat, and resumed his presentation. 'Honourable Apolo-Gyamfi has also drawn attention to the great compact between those who are living, those who are dead, and those who are to be born. Again his conception of these three levels of being is an echo of Edmund Burke, a great Anglo-Irishman, but not necessarily a great exponent of Africa's conception of this compact. The past, the present, and the future are not quite as unilinear as Edmund Burke and Kwame Apolo-Gyamfi seem to assume. We are dead and we are in After-Africa. Are we the past or the future or indeed the present? I suggest to the Elders of Judgement in all humility that what was absent from Apolo-Gyamfi's conception of the relationship between the living, the dead and those who are to be born was the simple and obvious principle of simultaneity. We here are discussing the Nigerian Civil War at a time when the same subject is being discussed, though in different contexts, by many on earth. In some respects the earth is indeed a Herebefore. And we are the "Hereafter" of those who are living. But we are the dead and the dead to those who are living are supposed to be part of the past. If we are in the "Hereafter", aren't we part of the future? Or are the past and the future no more than different sides of the coin of simultaneity?

'It is indeed true that for Africa art is also a compact between the living, the dead and those who are to be born, but certainly not in the Eurocentric terms which Apolo-Gyamfi has suggested. The mediating link in this great primaeval compact is precisely the specific society to which the African belongs. Art is a heritage from the past, honoured and augmented by the present, and then transmitted to the future. But the transmission is not unilinear, and the continuity is a social continuity. In Africa it is society which gives meaning to art. How then could Christopher Okigbo be deemed guilty for giving his life in the cause of his immediate society?

'In Africa the ancestors are kinsmen. The continuity between the dead and the living is a continuity of kinship. How then could Christopher Okigbo be regarded as a violator of the primaeval contract when he died in defence of the dignity of kinship?'

The Grand Stadium listened, sometimes impressed by the turn of an argument, occasionally irritated by excessive sophistication. But there was no doubt that Hamisi Salim was accepting the challenge of Apolo-Gyamfi at the level of discourse chosen by Apolo-Gyamfi himself.

Hamisi continued: 'I am also deeply disturbed by Apolo-Gyamfi's handling of the two concepts of life and art. Was Okigbo really supposed to value life for the sake of art? Was life to be valued purely as an instrument for the realization of art? Was there an antithesis between art and life?'

Here again the words of Okigbo suddenly filled the Stadium, willed into articulation by the process of Hamisi's reasoning, but the lines this time were not of poetry but of prose. It was the remark which Okigbo had made to Robert Serumaga in an interview in 1966.

'Poetry is not an alternative to living. It is only one way of supplementing life; and if I can live life to its fullest without writing at all, I don't care to write.'

A short silence followed before Hamisi continued: 'By dying for the Ibo, Okigbo had lived life to its fullest. It was right that he should not care to write.'

Hamisi then proceeded to enumerate the tragic antecedents to the Nigerian Civil War. He could see it all, the drift towards disintegration in 1964 and 1965; the sharpening of tribal positions; the politics of squalor; the rapid decay of the liberal ethos in the first four years of Nigeria's independence. Then came the *coup* of January 1966. It looked like a moment of delivery. Blood was spilt. The Nigerian *coup* was no glorious revolution. But there was an air of painful purification pervading that optimistic atmosphere of January 1966. Old scores were settled, ugly brutality reared its menacing head. And yet the first pen which was dipped into the blood of the victims of the first Nigerian *coup* proceeded to write on the white wall of destiny a single gory message – the word Hope!

'But it has not worked out,' continued Hamisi. 'The Ibo took the leadership in this great work of national salvage; but not all brave volunteers get decorated.'

The inevitable account of the mounting tension in Northern Nigeria then followed. The first great atrocities were recounted, a moment of vengeance by Northerners against bewildered Ibo. Ironsi, who had been catapulted to power by the first *coup*, had tried to rescue the situation with one last attempt at inter-tribal statesmanship. But the situation degenerated. A second *coup* swiftly sent Ironsi forth on his own great trek to After-Africa. He had arrived in After-Africa weary and perplexed. In the Herebefore, history had tried to thrust a greatness upon him, and for a moment he held that great burden in balance; but then his knees began to give way, and he asked his Ibo brother to lend him a hand. The burden of greatness, thrust on shoulders unequal to the task, took its toll. Ironsi stumbled into After-Africa, a monument of one of the great might-have-beens of history.

But whatever the deficiencies of leadership, nothing could forgive the carnage of September 1966. There had been a rumour that something ghastly was happening in the East. It was a broadcast picked up from a radio programme coming from outside the borders of Nigeria. The Ibo, the broadcast report claimed, were literally up in arms in the Eastern Region, cutting the throats of the Hausa. There were indeed Hausa tradesmen and even settlers in the East, and their presence had become a little precarious since the great events of May when the Ibo in Hausaland had sustained such casualties. But had the Ibo in the East risen in belated and ferocious retaliation?

'There is very little evidence to support such a thesis,' asserted Hamisi. Out on the hundred-and-seventy-third row Salisha caught her breath, covered her eyes and shook a little. Abiranja was sitting next to her. He reached out, put his hand on her knee and patted it in benevolent reassurance.

A number of other members of the audience had also turned to look at each other, and made brief comments in passing.

Hamisi was continuing: 'But in spite of this flimsy report of massacres against the Hausa coming from a foreign broadcast, the North nevertheless collectively uttered a shrill cry of indignation, reached for knives and swords, and proclaimed a *jihad* against a defenceless people.'

Hamisi swallowed at his own oratory. Brought up as a Muslim he had inhibitions about casting aspersions on fellow Muslims. He normally refrained from carelessly suspecting religious motives behind political brutalities. And he had himself shared the anger of many Muslims at Biafra's propaganda in trying to rally support for herself on a banner of Christian crusade. And yet here was he, Hamisi, in a battle to save the soul of a Biafran, wondering whether some of the suggestions of that old propaganda in the Herebefore might not be pertinent.

In his role as Counsel, Hamisi had a weakness which in great actors was a great strength. He had the capacity to identify so deeply with the cause he was espousing that his own responses became almost indistinguishable from those of prior partisans. On the stage Hamisi might have derived great resources of acting power by this compulsion to empathize. In the Grand Stadium of After-Africa, he was also drawing momentary advantage from the sheer sense of commitment which his identification

82

seemed to portray. The cold intellectual detachment of Kwame Apolo-Gyamfi on his feet was now decisively replaced by Hamisi in a mood of real political engagement.

He then used the device of citing case histories of a few Ibo victims of that September nightmare.

There was the case of Vincent Obika, the cobbler. Obika had lived in Kano for nineteen years. He had in many ways become assimilated into the life of the community, and conversed in the local language with exceptional fluency. He had also become sympathetic with many of the ways of the Hausa and Fulani, accepting the social distinctions with the resigned equanimity best exemplified among the British working-class in the Herebefore. Obika had attended many Muslim ceremonies, recognizing that as a non-Muslim he could not become a full participant, but accepting nevertheless that boundary of hospitality to aliens which the Northern ethos at its best afforded with regal allowance.

Obika had once in fact been married to a Hausa woman drawn from the lower classes. There were problems at the beginning arising from this mixed marriage, but after five years Obika's own philosophical equanimity won over even the strongest antagonist. His wife, Muna, bore him a son four years after their marriage, just at the time when both of them were getting desperate at the long period of barrenness.

Muna died of the great fever in 1963. Their son, Yunus, was then ten. Obika was deeply shaken by Muna's departure, and many in the neighbourhood were moved by his predicament. He became more attached than ever to Yunus.

But nature was still strong in Obika, and he needed another woman. This time he married a fellow Ibo, a young girl recently arrived from Port Harcourt. Again it was a relatively happy marriage, though less deep and intimate than Obika's first one. The new wife, affectionately called Sinjo, bore him one son and one daughter. Yunus was still the favourite, but no one begrudged such a clear eldest child the rights to active interaction with the father and the first option in moments of consultation.

And then that broadcast came in September. A fellow Ibo came to Obika's home, telling him of the slaughter which had begun. His wife, Sinjo, and his two younger children were visiting friends two miles away. Obika, the cobbler, by this time owned a car. He packed what he could, and then heard shouts outside his own house. He looked out – yes, they were coming from his own close neighbours and friends. There was a totally dehumanizing rage on their faces. He used the rear entrance and managed to open the garage, got into the car and started it before the approaching crowds knew what was happening. His son, Yunus, and the friend who had called got into the car in time. They drove off in a shower of stones, terrified and incredulous that some of their oldest and best friends in Kano should have worn that face of vengeance.

What about Sinjo and the children? Could they still be alive where they were? Obika swallowed in terror as he stepped on the accelerator.

18

Hamisi paused in his narration of the day of slaughter. He then turned to the Elders and said, 'Oh, my Elders, I crave indulgence to call into the witness box Vincent Obika.'

There was a stir in that massive auditorium. This simple cobbler was the first witness to be invited. He emerged from the North Gate, somewhat short, somewhat stout, greying at the temples and growing bald on top. He walked nervously towards the raised stage, and when he got there Hamisi guided him to the special *mihrab*, a pulpit-like construction, intended for witnesses. The *mihrab* was raised a little, and Obika climbed the three steps. He stumbled on the third, obviously a bundle of nerves and awkwardness.

Hamisi gave him time to regain his composure before he asked him to raise his arm – 'You swear to speak the truth, the whole truth, and nothing but the truth, so help you Fate?'

Obika, his bald patch beginning to shine with a thin film of perspiration, answered, 'I do.'

Hamisi said, 'You heard the tale I narrated to the Elders regarding that day of ugly vengeance in Kano. Were my facts correct?'

'Yes sir, they were.'

'Will you now tell the rest of the story to the wise Elders of Judgement,' Hamisi requested him.

Obika fidgeted, somewhat bewildered.

Hamisi said, 'You were in the car, having left your house, driving hard to find your wife Sinjo and your two younger children. Where were you going?'

Obika answered, 'To Udezue's house. The wife's relative, that's Udezue. The children go too.'

Obika stopped. Hamisi waited encouragingly. 'Go on.'

Obika gradually gathered momentum. 'I drove fair speed. My car was good, not too old. I got it by good bargain. But that day I needed it sharp. We drove hard we drove desperate.'

In his own unusual phraseology, Obika lent greater clarity to that agitated dash of theirs. At one corner he was recognized just as he was taking a turn, and a shout of hostility rang out. But they were well on their way, churning up the brown dust, throwing up a stone or two as the wheels spun in their fury.

They came at last to Udezue's street. There was a dead body at the beginning of the street – it might have been a Hausa man. There was a house burning further on. But Udezue's own relatively prosperous residence seemed serenely isolated from the terror of the moment. The lights were on on both floors, although it was not yet fully dark. Obika asked his fifteen year old son, Yunus, and the companion who had come to warn them of the riots, to remain in the car while he went to investigate quickly. Obika ran up the pathway, past the solitary and incongruous bougainvillaea, to the door of Udezue's home, painted a loud shade of green. The door was ajar. Obika called out. But there was no answer. He walked in carefully, almost tiptoeing. A sense of doom gripped him.

He looked into the huge room which Udezue used as his reception room for visiting Ibo brothers, Hausa friends, and customers. The room was in total disorder, much of the upholstery of the gaudy furniture ripped open, the cotton wool stuffing hanging out like the tongue of a thirsty dog on a hot day.

Obika gripped the handle of the door, trembling with terror. He was not a brave man. But he had to know.

He went up the steps softly, his heart pounding away, as much afraid of what he might see as for what might befall him. He got to the first floor, and witnessed yet more of the chaos of vandalism. But his worst fear focused on the great door of the main bedroom in the house, broken down and partly splintered, showing the signs of an axe at work. Obika felt a great urge to turn and run. Indeed he took two steps backwards. But he had to find out. Again he tiptoed a little closer. The main light in that room was broken, but for some reason there was a bedside lamp alight. It was that small, rather dim, almost peaceful light which revealed the gory details of Udezue's main bedroom. The entire group – Udezue, his wife, their one child, Sinjo, and Obika's two younger children – had retreated into the bedroom in a last bid for safety. But the vengeful intruders had followed them there, axed their way into the room, and left splintered bodies soaked in their own blood scattered amongst the debris of the bedroom furniture.

Obika stood there, anger, anguish, and horror all conspiring to throttle him. He stood there shaking, for there was a third element. The fear of a simple man afraid. He staggered to one side and was trying to regain his breath when he was startled once again into a sharp alertness. It was the shouting of a crowd outside. Were they after him? He was trying to think where to hide when he suddenly remembered Yunus in the car. The shouting got louder. Obika turned round and ran down the steps, shouting 'Yunus!' He stumbled on to an empty bucket, sending it crashing to the side wall. He ran out of the door down the pathway, and to his horror saw his own car aflame. There was a crowd around it and great shouting. He ran near; the crowd had not noticed him. In the car he saw the two faces, Yunus and his companion, unconscious, bleeding from their foreheads. They had obviously been brutally knocked on the head, possibly as they were trying to get out of the car and run. Then, unconscious, they had both been bundled back into the car. The doors had been shut, and with incredible viciousness, they were now being cremated alive. It was clearly too late to save them, yet Obika, forgetting his own vulnerability, pushed his way through. In all that din, he was shouting 'Yunus, Yunus!' The crowd had still not realized that they had an Ibo in their midst. Obika got near; the flames were too hot, so he covered his face and retreated. As he turned round he saw one man laughing. It was all he needed. All his agony, all his fear, all his timidity somehow underwent a transformation into a rage such as he had never experienced before. He jumped on the man who was laughing, reached for his throat, pulled him to the ground and started bashing his head, shouting 'Hausa dog, Hausa dog!' Shortly he started feeling arms trying to pull him away from the man, sticks hitting him, the sharp sting of a stab on his right shoulder. But Obika kept on throttling. The head of his victim bashed, bleeding, mixed with the brown dust, kept up the tempo of Obika's retribution. The victim was dead but Obika kept on, throttling, and hitting the head on to the ground, screaming 'Hausa dog! Hausa dog!'

Obika himself was now bleeding profusely, his energies were ebbing, but his hands were still tight round the neck. He saw Yunus five years previously throwing a ball for him to catch. He felt a hammer in his hand, repairing an old shoe, hitting at the last rusty nail. He heard the voice of his first wife, Muna, proclaiming that the midday food was ready. He hit the nail more ferociously for speed; he held the shoe tight – it was the neck of his dead victim – he throttled once more.

In that *mihrab* in the Grand Stadium, Obika was holding on to one of the ornamented pillars of the witness-box throttling it, sobbing with rage, reliving that evening of vengeance with the words 'Hausa dog! Hausa dog!'

Hamisi went up the steps into the witness-box, and put his hand softly on Obika's shoulder. Obika gradually stopped, looked at

Hamisi, tears running down his old cheeks. He realized where he was, calmed down a little, and was gradually reduced to his usual nervous timidity.

Hamisi asked Apolo-Gyamfi if he had any questions to ask the witness. Apolo-Gyamfi shook his head. Hamisi helped Obika down, and accompanied him part of the way towards the North Gate. Echoes of his cry 'Hausa dog!' still lingered in the consciousness of the audience. An Ibo killing a Hausa man by the side of his own son sizzling in a live cremation, and the evening sky of Nigeria mocking the scene below.

Suddenly in that Grand Stadium, as Hamisi was accompanying Obika towards the North Gate, the House was once again called to attention. Hamisi and Obika stopped in their steps. The Elders of Judgement sat up in their thrones. It was Okigbo's poetry, evoking the image of the Nigerian evening sky mocking the scene of an Ibo throttling a Hausa in the light of a burning car. The voice filled that judicial cosmos with the words:

> *The moon has ascended between us,*
> *Between two pines*
> *That bow to each other;*
>
> *Love with the moon has ascended,*
> *Has fed on our solitary stems;*
>
> *And we are now shadows*
> *That cling to each other,*
> *But kiss the air only.*

A silence reigned in the Grand Stadium. Hamisi walked back to the stage of the trial. He let the message of the story of the cobbler sink in. Then he resumed his argument against Apolo-Gyamfi.

How could it be suggested that Okigbo's conversion to the cause of Ibo separatism was a denial of universal values? It was true that a great writer had a duty which went beyond his own society, but it was not a duty which transcended that society. There were national agonies which demanded full engagement, especially from the most gifted of the members of that nation.

Nor was it to be assumed that Okigbo's resort to arms was necessarily a disservice to Nigeria, simply because it was a commitment to Biafra. A blood-stained Nigeria might claim to be one Nigeria, but it could hardly claim to be indivisible. The Nigerians themselves needed to be saved from their folly – for they knew not what they were doing. 'By attempting to save his people, the Ibo, Okigbo was in a profound sense also attempting to save his people's enemies.'

The writer in Africa, asserted Hamisi, needed to be socially committed if he was to be universally engaged. As one African intellectual had once put it, social commitment was not to be confused with social conformity. When African regimes, like the Federal one, asked their writers to be concerned with the nation, it was important to refrain from equating national concern with political convenience. A writer could be committed by opposing the folly of his government, or the intolerance of his society. Wole Soyinka, the Nigerian playwright, had done precisely that when he expressed his reservations about his government's policy towards the Ibo.

Hamisi here said: 'But let Soyinka speak for himself. Oh, Elders of Judgement, I call upon the voice of Wole Soyinka, a son of Nigeria, to testify in these proceedings.'

A moment passed, thunder again shattered the momentary stillness of the Grand Stadium, and then the words of Soyinka descended resonant into the auditorium.

Poets have lately taken to gun-running and others are accused of holding up radio stations. In several independent states the writer is part of some underground movement; one coup at least in Africa is reputed to have involved a novelist and a poet ... Where the writer in his own society can no longer function as conscience he must recognize that his choice lies between denying himself totally or withdrawing to the position of chronicler and post-mortem surgeon. But there can be no

further distraction with universal concerns whose balm is
spread on abstract wounds, not in the gaping yaws of black
inhumanity . . . The artist has always functioned in his society
as the record of mores and experience of his society and as the
voice of vision in his own time. It is time for him to respond to
this essence of himself.

Soyinka's resonant testimony, summoned from the Herebefore,
came to an end. Hamisi took the argument further with the
words: 'It was precisely to that essence of himself that Okigbo
responded. To fight for universals is to concretize literature – and
the fight in Biafra was indeed such a fight.'

Apolo-Gyamfi had asserted that by dying, Okigbo had killed his
own poetry. Hamisi retorted: 'How wrong is such a view.
Okigbo's death was itself a piece of poetry at its deepest.'

And almost in moving testimony of support, the Stadium heard
once again Okigbo's own lines reaffirming:

> *When you have finished*
> *& done up my stitches,*
> *Wake me near the altar,*
> *& this poem will be finished . . .*

19

Hamisi was having a late supper quietly with Abiranja. It had
been a hard day at the Grand Stadium, though on balance Hamisi
had clearly made an unexpected impact. His use of evidence from
witnesses had been adroitly selective. His choice of the Ibo
cobbler as one of his star witnesses was itself a brilliant move.
Much of the Ibo's story belonged more to the realm of pathos than
to real tragedy, but there were aspects of high human drama at its
most agonizing. That scene by the burning car – a case not only of
timidity conquered by simple indignation, but a case also of tragic

ambiguities. An angry Ibo man was throttling a Hausa man by the side of a car in flames. Within the car was the sizzling body of a fifteen-year-old child, half Ibo, half Hausa.

And as the father was throttling a bystander in revenge, and shouting 'Hausa dog! Hausa dog!' he could still hear the voice of his first wife, a Hausa woman, beckoning him home to come and have his food. Muna, long deceased, lovingly keeping her Ibo husband company in his last outrage against the Hausa.

But perhaps too much reflection on tragedy reduces its tragic dimensions. High human drama of that kind is to be felt in imaginative ambiguity, rather than analysed with intellectual precision. Or is it?

Hamisi and Abiranja had together been conducting a post-mortem on the day's proceedings in Court. It was improper for Hamisi to discuss the coming moves with anyone, but there was no objection to the idea of examining what had already transpired.

Hamisi had been initially somewhat terrified of having to engage in a battle of wits with Kwame Apolo-Gyamfi. Some intellectuals acquire such a reputation that, inadvertently, they let loose a variety of inhibiting complexes on many of their prospective rivals. But when the confrontation actually takes place the odds are seldom as great as originally expected. The imagined disparities between the minds reduce themselves to manageable proportions.

Abiranja mentioned casually that Apolo-Gyamfi should not be underestimated. It was the nearest that Abiranja came to tendering any advice to Hamisi about the later conduct of the trial. The simple point was made after careful deliberation by Abiranja in order to determine whether or not it fell within the bounds of judicial propriety. Abiranja's experience as an immortal helped to guide him in this delicate game of testing the limits of legitimate advice.

Hamisi asked, 'But it is proper, is it not, to talk a little more about Apolo-Gyamfi's background? What did happen at Oxford?'

As the two finished their dessert they talked about Oxford in wartime, the improvisations which had to be made, the sense of nearness to London and its needs and losses as a major target of enemy bombing; the concern for children moved out of the capital; the general commitment by this seat of aristocratic enlightenment to the needs of the nation.

But the intellectual exchanges and debates still went on in wartime Oxford, sometimes serious, but more often with characteristic, if sophisticated, frivolity. An event which caused a particular sensation both in After-Europe and After-Africa was the Oxford Union debate on the motion 'This House believes that to die for king and country is an exercise in futility'. The debate ended in uproar, with a degree of juvenile violence more in keeping with the mood of a nation at war than with the tradition of this retreat of meditation. And yet, perhaps even violence was part of the fabric of the Oxford tradition.

Before the final uproar, Kwame Apolo-Gyamfi had spoken from the floor in that debate. It was his maiden speech in the Oxford Union, and became the starting-point in a dazzling student career. It was not just Britain which was at war at that time; it was, of course, the rest of the British Empire as well. Apolo-Gyamfi spoke from the perspective of the colonial. His was the most significant contribution in that debate from the point of view of those who were dragged into the war, not because they were British citizens, but because they were British colonial subjects. Apolo-Gyamfi had referred to the smug observation which Winston Churchill as Prime Minister had recently made:

Three years ago, all over the world, friend and foe alike – everyone who had not the eye of faith – might well have deemed our speedy ruin at hand. Against the triumphant might of Hitler, with the greedy Italians at his tail, we stood alone with resources so slender that one shudders to enumerate them now. Then, surely, was the moment for the Empire to break up, for each of its widely-dispersed communities to seek safety on the winning side, for those who thought themselves oppressed

to throw off their yoke and make better terms betimes with the
all-conquering Nazi and Fascist power. Then was the time. But
what happened?

Apolo-Gyamfi invoked the answer given by Lugard, one of the
great architects of Nigeria as an imperial creation. In 1941 Lugard
was already in a position to praise Africans for 'the loyalty they
have shown in this, as in the last war, by readiness to serve in the
field and by gifts often pathetic in their simplicity towards the
cost of the war or to Red Cross funds'. Africa had indeed appeared
to respond to what Churchill described as 'the trumpet call of a
supreme crisis'. Then, amid uproar, Apolo-Gyamfi said he was
sometimes ashamed to see simple African tribesmen devote much
needed heads of cattle to a British war effort, or an old African
come to the District Commissioner with a basket of eggs to help
Bwana Churchill.

Apolo-Gyamfi, amid further uproar, asserted that he had found
much to admire in Subhas Bose, the Indian nationalist, who had
tried to form a 'Free India Army' with the slogan of 'Asia for the
Asians', dedicated to fight on the side of the Japanese against
British imperial power.

But although Apolo-Gyamfi would agree with the spirit of
Subhas Bose's resistance, he was not sure he would accept the
nature of his tactics. With staggering cynicism, Apolo-Gyamfi said
there was a case for fighting on the British side, even if one was a
colonial – not in order to make Britain win necessarily, but in
order to help prolong the war. A Britain isolated in the face of
Nazi strength might have capitulated all too quickly. The Nazis
would then have been much stronger and more able to exercise
their hegemony over what had previously been British domains.
Nazi imperial rule was, without question, bound to be less
humane and more racialistic than British rule had ever been.

If the choice had indeed been simply between British rule and
German rule under the Nazis, he as an African would without a
moment's hesitation opt for the banner of King George. But the
most promising prospect for the colonial peoples was not a swift

victory by one over the other, but a prolonged conflict which would leave both victor and vanquished too exhausted to remain a great imperial power. To support the Germans at that time would indeed bring the conflict rapidly to a close, since it was the Germans who were stronger in any case. But to support the weaker side in the war was a contribution towards its prolongation.

There stood this short little African from the Gold Coast, with boos and cheers intermingling in reaction to his analysis, not faltering in his fluency in spite of the uproar surrounding him, maintaining a posture of dignified cynicism worthy of the highest traditions of Oxford.

'Yes, I am sometimes ashamed to read about a grey-haired fellow countryman contributing a basket of eggs to the District Commissioner to help Britain with her breakfast problems. And yet I see a logic in this as well. It is indeed in our interest to help Britain get back on her feet in the boxing-ring after every brutal round. We are her hands in this great bout with Germany. On balance we would rather see Britain win than see her opponent take the final call of applause. But even more preferable is a prolonged boxing-match that will leave both contenders exhausted at the end of it all, and incapable of bullying their weaker entourage much longer.'

It was a great performance by Apolo-Gyamfi. Many patriotic British students who were shocked by the sentiments he was expressing, were nevertheless impressed by the cruelty of Apolo-Gyamfi's Oxonian wit. Indian, Malay, and fellow African students were loudly behind him as he hammered home his points. A large section of British opinion in the debate heckled and booed some of his views. A few even uttered racialistic obscenities at Apolo-Gyamfi. But his dignified resilience as he held the floor was a memorable performance in the annals of the Oxford Union.

In the following year Apolo-Gyamfi stood for President of the Union. It was a sensational contest, against the son of a well-known aristocratic Scottish family. Apolo-Gyamfi, in spite of the deep controversy which had surrounded his speech in the debate, and in spite of the continuing atmosphere of patriotic fervour in wartime Britain, nearly won the election. He missed the opportunity of being the first African President of the Oxford Union by less than half a dozen votes. There were two recounts before the final victory was announced. The nearness of Apolo-Gyamfi's victory was in itself historic.

The third year came and the examinations were due. He reverted to his work habits and prepared himself. Ever since his success in the essay competition in the Gold Coast when he was fourteen, Apolo-Gyamfi had basked in popular admiration in much of West Africa as a budding intellectual. He was expected to do brilliantly throughout his studies and return to Ghana as an intellectual luminary of the first order. Inevitably Apolo-Gyamfi began to feel the push of popular expectation as he went through life from stage to stage. He had wanted at first to do well for his own sake; then to do well for the sake of his family; but now he had to do well for the sake of his fans. He had until then pulled it off. He had been on top form throughout his school career, winning almost every prize. He had then sailed into Oxford with ease. The question which arose was whether he would shine as well in an English university as he had done in West African schools. The old idea that the real test comes when a person is in competition with white minds was still an important feature of popular calculation in the Africa of the 1940s.

Apolo-Gyamfi's exams came. He did eleven of his papers with full satisfaction to himself, but he was startled by the twelfth. It was a curious case of a conspiracy of destiny. The very fact that it was the last paper put a touch of ironic neatness to the whole story.

Apolo-Gyamfi staggered out of the examination room, convinced that he had failed his twelfth paper. The agony built up only slowly, as he reflected on the impact it would have on his family and on those who had expected so much out of his Oxford career. If he had failed his twelfth paper, there was still the chance that he had passed the rest of his papers. But what worried Apolo-Gyamfi was the idea of not getting a First in his examinations. Oxford had an undifferentiated Second Class degree. All who failed to get a First got either a Second or a Third. The idea of an Upper or a Lower Second was regarded as a refinement of no important significance. To miss a First for Apolo-Gyamfi was a prospect too painful to contemplate for any length of time.

Apolo-Gyamfi locked himself up in his rooms at the College for much of the rest of the day.

He could not remember at what stage in the late afternoon he decided to go out and buy a couple of bottles of whisky from his tutor's black-market contact, but it was to these bottles that he resorted as a fairly conventional solution to his depression. He drank a lot on an empty stomach. It was around ten-thirty in the evening when some of his neighbours in College heard him staggering out. He went down the stairway and emerged into the damp, dreary, and very dark Oxford night. He struggled and got his motor-cycle out. Jonathan Wilton, an Australian student at the College, tried to stop him going out. Apolo-Gyamfi was clearly drunk and in no state to ride his motor-cycle. But for his pains Wilton got a swinging, unsteady but hard, punch on the chin. Wilton dashed back into the College quadrangle looking for help. Apolo-Gyamfi had to be stopped. As Wilton stood near the East Pond of the quadrangle, uncertain whom to call out to, he suddenly heard Apolo-Gyamfi's motor-cycle starting. He dashed back to the College gate shouting, 'Stop! Stop, Kwame!' But Apolo-Gyamfi's motor-cycle had started. The wartime policy of 'Black-Out' was still in force, and vehicles were supposed to have only parking lights on. Apolo-Gyamfi's motor-cycle had no lights on whatsoever as he moved rather noisily in the direction of Corn-market. Wilton stared helplessly as the ominous noise was swallowed up by the darkness.

News spread in College the following day. Kwame Apolo-Gyamfi was dead. His body was found not far from Rhodes House. It was not clear what he had hit in those dark streets of wartime Oxford. It might have been something relatively small which threw him off course, made him swerve into a pavement, and sent him plunging to his lonely death. His neck was broken.

His friends at Oxford, his family in the Gold Coast, and all those fans he had, did not know for certain why Apolo-Gyamfi had behaved in such a manner that night. The fact that he normally drank very little was something which received wide publicity after his death. It added to the mystery of his behaviour. As he had locked himself up in his room and had been drinking furiously after his last examination paper at Oxford, people at first thought it must have been connected with his performance in the examinations. Yet, when the results came out, Apolo-Gyamfi had a First Class – one of the best First Class performances at Oxford that year. It was certainly the best in his subject. Why had Apolo-Gyamfi behaved so inexplicably on the eve of the crowning achievement of his academic career? Might he have been in doubt about the level of his performance?

Abiranja poured himself a little more port. He continued, 'His folk in the Herebefore remained mystified about the causes of Kwame's behaviour on his last day of life. In After-Africa Apolo-Gyamfi's accident made an impact; he was going to be tried at first.'

Hamisi asked, 'Was he going to be charged for his vanity? For his inflated obsession with a First Class degree?'

Abiranja replied, 'No, ambition is not a major sin. Nor is pride, in spite of the earthly versions of the fall of Satan. The real crime committed by Apolo-Gyamfi was the sin of impatience. Having decided that he could not have done well in his final paper, and having inferred from that that he was no longer in the running for a First Class degree, he might at least have had the patience to test his speculations against the facts. He might have waited for the results before deciding to lock himself up in his rooms, seeking the solace of the bottle.'

'What a waste!' Hamisi heard himself commenting. But he wondered about the propriety of such reflections when looking at death from this side of the border.

He rose from his chair, somewhat laboriously, and groaned. 'I need exercise. Maybe I should join one of those football teams!' He laughed, and then his eyes betrayed a sudden recollection of something long forgotten. He sat down again.

'There was something else I wanted to ask you, Abiranja. I had great help in my initial investigations from a Nigerian called Jacob Alobi. I went to see him at the Stadium not long after that soccer match, and he gave me some useful insights into certain aspects of the Nigerian Civil War, of Christopher Okigbo himself, and of some of the personal factors at play in the situation. He also gave me a number of other names to consult, and this greatly strengthened my basic knowledge of Nigeria on the eve of the trial.'

Abiranja said, 'Yes, I know Alobi. He is a vivacious and dynamic creature, full of talk but also capable of action.'

'But what was he doing in the football team of the Sixteenth Century if he was killed in the Nigerian Civil War in the twentieth century?'

Abiranja answered, 'It is connected with how he died – let me try and remember.'

There was a moment of silence, as Abiranja strained to recall a small corner of his memory. The frown of concentration gradually eased, and his eyes betrayed the quiet gratification of rediscovery.

'Oh yes – Alobi tried to strangle a priest in prayer. It happened when their plane was on fire and losing height rapidly. They were all clearly doomed, and the priest was on his knees in passionate if somewhat frightened communion with his Maker. Alobi was suddenly incensed by this spectacle and he jumped and caught hold of the priest's throat shouting "Shut up! Shut up!" '

Hamisi waited to see the connection between this and playing for the Sixteenth Century. Abiranja came to the connection. 'In punishment for brutalizing those who are frightened into prayer, the Elders of After-Africa decided that Alobi must be tried by the canons of the Spanish Inquisition which was at its most elaborate in the sixteenth century, just before its final collapse.' But the Elders also felt that there were certain mitigating circumstances in the situation, and it would therefore be too harsh to expect Alobi to defend himself before an Inquisition without prior initiation into the ways of thought of the sixteenth century. He was therefore permitted to apply to the Grand Council of the Sixteenth Century for dispensation to participate in some of the activities of the century. After elaborate discussions, Alobi did at last receive the message of dispensation from the Grand Council. He was allowed to be an associate member of the Thursday Club of the sixteenth century, specializing in keeping alive certain special dances of that period. He was also given full dining rights to the Sunset Cauldron, the best place for sixteenth-century cuisine with a variety drawn from Mediterranean civilizations to the food culture of the Hottentots. But above all Alobi, who had played for Nigeria in the Herebefore, was permitted the status of full player in the Sixteenth Century Eleven.

The Inquisition had not yet taken place. But until it did, Alobi enjoyed a variety of privileges within a century significantly removed from his own. What would happen at the Inquisition was not clear. The possibility of elaborate torturing methods, which were at once a trial and a punishment, was not ruled out where the occasion justified it in After-Africa. Nor could the notion of being sentenced to hell-fire be discounted. There was such a place as hell-fire, in After-Africa, but only a small minority of serious offenders were ever sentenced to it. No one stayed there eternally. The nature of the treatment ranged from serving a sentence of four decades in a Turkish bath to serving a sentence of several centuries in what was known as the eternal crematorium.

Hamisi felt that at the worst Alobi could only be sentenced to four decades of a Turkish bath. And if he were so sentenced Hamisi was sure he would make a deal with the warder to provide him with one massage girl to practise her fingers on his long shiny limbs as he lay prostrate and suggestively naked in a cloud of Ottoman steam.

Hamisi made another attempt to rise. 'It has been a fascinating evening, Abiranja,' Hamisi said. 'But I must go and give a little further thought to tomorrow's proceedings before I hit the mattress for the night.'

Abiranja also rose. 'Yes, you must go and do your homework

before you confront the Elders and Apolo-Gyamfi once again tomorrow. I hope you have more surprises for us.'

Hamisi laughed. 'We'll see,' he said. 'Good night. Abiranja.'

'Good night.'

20

The hum of expectancy echoed from the tall columns of the Grand Stadium. The crowds were resuming their seats for the continuation of the trial of Christopher Okigbo. Some were talking about the proceedings of the previous day, some were exchanging greetings, some were sighing for things to come. 'I haven't seen you for a century,' a voice was shouting to a friend across the gangway.

At last the herald of the Elders' arrival sounded out. Stillness descended once again on the Grand Stadium. The Elders marched with elegant deliberation towards their nine thrones.

The Counsels then appeared from their two corners, marched towards each other, and then shoulder to shoulder found their way back to the Stage of Decision. They stood to attention, waiting to receive, from the Elder on the fifth throne, permission to resume the proceedings. An important dimension of the suspense of that day was the simple issue of which witnesses would be called by the two Counsels. There was a general belief in After-Africa that the most obvious witnesses were not necessarily the most relevant witnesses. No one really expected Ironsi, the head of the first military junta in Nigeria, to be called to the witness-box. No one expected Sir Abubakar Tafawa Balewa or the Sardauna of Sokoto to make an appearance during the proceedings. They were indeed pertinent figures in the great drama which had led to the Nigerian Civil War, but their very centrality in that drama made them suspect as witnesses. It was not their integrity which was under a cloud; it was merely a feeling that the centre of affairs had already had too much attention and tended to divert adequate examination of the periphery. The tendency in the grand trials of After-Africa was to seek the less obvious witnesses in the belief that the deeper probing which would be needed to establish their relevance would itself be a way of exploring more extensively for critical links of pertinence. Indeed, the witnesses called need have very little to do with the Nigerian Civil War. Part of the artistry of legal oratory and cross-examination on the Stage of Decision lay in unearthing the depths of meaning in otherwise simple events and the hidden links in otherwise disparate phenomena.

The multitudes waited. The signal came from the Elder on the fifth throne. Hamisi was seated, and Apolo-Gyamfi stood and said, 'I call for Pete Kawesa!'

There was some discussion in the audience, as it was not a famous name and certainly did not sound West African, let alone Nigerian.

Pete Kawesa walked across the field with a great show of deliberation. He was enjoying every minute of the attention that was rivetted on his little figure as he approached the Platform of Decision. He was a simple man, with simple ideas of grandeur. In his own way he had suffered a little in the Herebefore, but he enjoyed the fun of being talked about. He was just over five feet, a little plump, lips somewhat thin, eyebrows decidedly bushy. His moustache was well looked after, neatly trimmed and perfectly symmetrical. The nostrils turned outwards, and one would have expected them to be rather hairy given the indications of Kawesa's hairy arms and bushy eyebrows. But if his nostrils were normally hairy the scissors had been delicately at work, breath suspended while the path was cleared.

Counsel for Damnation signalled Pete Kawesa on to the witness-stand. He made him take the oath, 'I swear to speak the truth, the whole truth, and nothing but the truth, so help me Fate!'

Apolo-Gyamfi then proceeded to ask Pete Kawesa a few questions to establish his identity. He was a Muganda, a taxi driver by profession, and met his death on December 19th, 1969.

Pete Kawesa was permitted to give his evidence in Luganda. No special gadgets for simultaneous translation were needed in After-Africa. Those who did not understand Luganda received the translation in the language of their preference just by an act of will, independent of switches and the glass cubicles of interpreters. Kawesa spoke in Luganda, and the multitude heard him in a variety of languages. Each listener privately alerted his own ear to the code of his choice. The Nigerian cobbler in his evidence had, for reasons perhaps connected with the terror of being identified as an Ibo on that last day of his in the Herebefore, chosen to speak in halting English, but Pete Kawesa's English was too inadequate to be admissible. Although he too had a lingering terror of being easily identifiable as a Muganda, he had to fall back on his own language for effective recapitulation of the events of his last days on earth.

It was a simple story. He was a taxi driver, well versed in the art of taking people for a ride in more senses than one.

Among his friends was Ali Mayanja, another taxi driver. They had known each other for years, and had once even tried jointly to form a trade union of taxi drivers for Eastern Africa. It was an ambitious venture, and gradually narrowed itself down to a trade union for Uganda taxi drivers, and then even further down to a trade union for Kampala taxi drivers. If a comparison were drawn of the two, Ali Mayanja would clearly stand out as the more intelligent, and in many ways the more attractive personality. But Pete was not without some compensating qualities, including a great capacity for hard work, and some genius in elementary strategy.

Pete Kawesa had sometimes borrowed money from Mayanja, but seldom paid him back. Mayanja himself liked the man, and normally said that he was keeping account of every cent that Pete Kawesa had taken, waiting for the day when Pete's crafty temperament would finally hit the jackpot and earn him a fortune. On occasions, when business was slack and Mayanja needed some money, he would bully Pete Kawesa into drawing upon his savings to pay back a little of what he owed. But the main thing was that they enjoyed each other's company, and made allowances for each other's faults – though Pete had more faults and Mayanja made more allowances.

Sometime in the second half of 1968 Mayanja acquired a new mistress at Wandegeya. They became quite close, and Mayanja gave up some of his older and more boisterous pleasures in order to concentrate on the seductive companionship of Lolia.

Mayanja did take Pete Kawesa home to Lolia's for lunch once or twice. He was normally rather wary about introducing his girl-friends to Pete Kawesa, not because he thought Pete Kawesa was more eligible, but because he felt Pete might embarrass the girl-friends by making advances all the same.

But nothing really happened on this front until that black Friday of December 1969. Mayanja had a customer who wanted to go all the way to Kabale. It was a great opportunity to make a neat package, as the passenger was a lecturer at Makerere University College. Mayanja saw Kawesa at the taxi rank in Wandegeya before departure that morning. They were in good humour. Mayanja and his academic customer left for Kabale before noon on December 19th.

At four-thirty Kawesa turned up at Lolia's place. He said that Mayanja had asked him to call and see if everything was all right. Mayanja had, so Kawesa claimed, even suggested that it might be a good idea to take Lolia to a dance at the New Life Club that night just to keep her amused. Lolia had not been to a dance for quite a while, as Mayanja was not a great dancer. It was therefore tempting to accept the suggestion. But had Mayanja really suggested it? It might have been Mayanja's guilty conscience for having failed to take her out often enough to places like the New Life Club.

Mayanja had been loyal to the name of Kawesa in discussing him with Lolia. Lolia had no idea about some of the reservations Mayanja had regarding Kawesa's character.

They went to the New Life Club that night, danced a lot, and drank even more. By eleven o'clock Lolia was far too drunk to be of much use on the dance floor any longer. Mayanja's relative temperance, and the new possessiveness that had afflicted him and made him keep Lolia at home instead of making her share the old boisterous life he used to lead, had to some extent reduced Lolia to a bundle of frustration. Mayanja was excellent in bed, and looked after her financially with great generosity. That side of it was all right. But she missed those long sessions with beer, or even *waragi*, that she used to enjoy with other men before she met Mayanja.

Soon after eleven, they left the New Life Club and staggered into Kawesa's Volkswagen. Kawesa was still sober enough to know his way, and indeed to know what he wanted for the rest of the evening. He was trying to make up his mind whether to take Lolia to his own place, or to spend the night with her at her place. He decided that there was greater risk in spending the night at his own place, as Maria, his regular girl-friend, might easily turn up on a Friday night however late. But Mayanja, they knew, was nearly three hundred miles away. He was expected to return from Kabale the following evening at the earliest.

They arrived at Lolia's place safely. Kawesa locked up his taxi, with Lolia standing by him unsteadily, giggling as he tried to fit the key into the hole.

He took her in, helped her to undress, and helped her to the lavatory to let her piss on the floor.

Then, arms round each other's shoulders, giggling away, they stumbled back into the bedroom. Kawesa put her on the bed, and stood and undressed himself in the dim light of Lolia's room. After that, he removed the remaining items of clothing on Lolia's body – the bra came off first, next the sweaty pants. He left the cheap gaudy necklace hanging round her neck, forming a pattern of some kind between her two breasts. Kawesa proceeded to make love to Lolia twice, each a prolonged session. Then exhausted, they both lay naked and fell asleep.

Kawesa, in the witness-box on the Stage of Decision, admitted that he could not recollect precisely at what time they were jolted out of their slumber in frightened response to a terrific banging on the outside door.

'It must be Ali Mayanja back already!' exclaimed Kawesa.

They were not quite sure what to do. He had time only to put his shirt on, unbuttoned, when Lolia pushed him under the bed. She was afraid the door would be knocked down, and that she might have to pay from her own savings for its repair.

'Wait, wait,' she shouted as she hurriedly covered herself with a sheet. 'Wait Ali!'

But when she opened the door it wasn't Ali Mayanja who confronted her. It was a couple of soldiers in uniform and armed. One of them caught hold of her wrist and dragged her in while the other had his revolver in readiness as they searched the little dwelling. Pete Kawesa was dragged out from under Lolia's bed, his shirt on but unbuttoned in front, the rest of him naked. There were tell-tale sticky white marks round his hairy nakedness, evidence of this evening of betrayal. As they were dragging him out of the room towards the outside Kawesa was protesting, 'Tell Ali I won't do it again! Why didn't he come himself? Tell him I won't do it again.'

He was protesting in agitated Luganda, while one of the soldiers dragged him by the scruff of his neck shouting in Swahili, '*Nyamaza! Wacha kelele!*' The first soldier let his comrade deal with Kawesa while he returned to the bedroom. Lolia's sheet was falling off her, and she was trying to cover herself again. The soldier crossed the threshhold, and closed the door behind him. A minute later, as Lolia stiffly received the soldier into her body, they heard two shots outside.

Apolo-Gyamfi paused in his probing examination to let the story sink in. He turned to Kawesa, the witness, and asked, 'Did you know what had happened that night at Lugogo Stadium in Kampala?'

Kawesa answered, 'I did not know till I arrived in After-Africa that an attempt had been made on President Obote's life!'

'Why did you think the soldier was dragging you out? As you watched his revolver aiming at you what passed through your mind?'

Kawesa said, 'I was confused, but the only crime I could think of was my betrayal of Ali Mayanja. I could not quite see why Mayanja, a fellow Muganda, should have employed Northern soldiers to come and deal with me. But that was the only crime I could think of. I never had time to work it out.'

The Grand Stadium waited for Apolo-Gyamfi to draw the final moral from the story of Pete Kawesa and his friend's mistress.

Apolo-Gyamfi cast his eyes at the audience in the Grand Stadium slowly and expressively. He turned his eyes back towards the Elders and said, 'Oh, my Elders of Judgement, in the story of this wretch, Kawesa, is the agony of our continent in the Here-before. The Ibo in Nigeria have said that they had a right to secede because the Government of Nigeria could not guarantee them security of life. Who has security in the Africa of this generation? The Ibo in Nigeria were at their most arrogant when they claimed the right to safety.'

The present generation of Africans was sentenced to the anguish of uncertainty, from one day to the next. When the Ibo claimed that they had a right to secede because they could not be guaranteed security, they in fact had more security within their homeland than the Baganda had in Buganda. It was true that the Ibo in the Northern Region and elsewhere in the old Federation were exposed. The enormous casualty rate of the Northern riots clearly testified to Ibo vulnerability outside Iboland. But once they returned to their ancestral starting-point, and consolidated themselves in Iboland in a bargaining position with the Central Government, their position was substantially stronger than that of the Baganda in Uganda. The critical differentiating variable was that while the Ibo remained a significant part of the Nigerian armed forces, the Baganda had boycotted the profession of soldiering. When flattered during the colonial period by British favours, they had retreated into a state of demilitarized arrogance.

But Apolo-Gyamfi conceded that there was a brighter side to this demilitarized state of Buganda. Because the Baganda, unlike the Ibo, had not controlled a substantial part of the armed forces of their country on attainment of independence, Uganda had been spared the kind of war which Ibo military self-confidence had released on to the people of Biafra and Nigeria.

'In other words, it might well be a blessing in disguise that the

Baganda are sufficiently demilitarized that they have no alternative but to accept central authority and gradual merging with the Ugandan nation. The Baganda have had a longer tradition of separatism than the Ibo, and might have made a bid to secede with less provocation than the Ibo needed.'

Apolo-Gyamfi paused, and looked at Pete Kawesa; then he turned, looked at the audience, and resumed his address facing the Elders.

'Yes, my Elders, the Ibo in Nigeria were at their most arrogant when they claimed the right to safety in the Africa of their day. In that Africa each sunrise was bound to be a question-mark, each sunset a speculation.'

A cobbler's neighbours in Kano could suddenly change, transformed by a single broadcast from a foreign country into militant tribal antagonists. A couple of soldiers in Wandegeya, Kampala, could divide between themselves a bed of pleasure and a backyard of execution. Neither the neighbours of the cobbler nor the two soldiers in Kampala were necessarily symbols of wickedness. They were merely signposts on a long and arduous highroad.

That Grand Stadium had heard a great debate before, on the fortunes of the Congo after 1960. Another African soldier had been tried for sparking off a mutiny with momentous consequences for his country. But the Congo, Nigeria, and Uganda were simply fragments of an African mirror. In between the cracks of the mirror the pattern of a continent emerged.

'Yes,' said Apolo-Gyamfi, 'death is indeed an exercise in pan-Africanism. We have been known to kill each other partly because we belong to each other. We kill each other because we are neighbours.'

Apolo-Gyamfi paused again, and resumed his level and expressive regard of the audience.

The witness Kawesa was released from the Pulpit of Evidence. His recollection, in his evidence, of that night of terror had unnerved him somewhat. But as he got down the steps from the Stage of Decision and walked across the field, he became once again aware that he was a conspicuous presence in a vast arena. He liked the sensation, and changed his gait once more to a jaunty, self-confident stride.

When attention had at last reverted to the Stage of Decision, the still figure of Apolo-Gyamfi resumed its discourse. Counsel said that he had seriously considered summoning to the witness-box Thomas Joseph Mboya, recently deceased from Kenya. He would have been a relevant witness, both from the point of view of illustrating another dimension of tragic uncertainties in Africa, but also in order to present a personality of political integration comparable to Ukpabi Asika, the Ibo who remained actively loyal to Nigeria. Both Asika and Mboya had to be regarded as integrationist heroes, in their capacity to transcend their ethnic affiliations for bigger causes.

At this point Hamisi got up to lodge an objection.

'If Counsel wants to invite either Mr Mboya in person or the voice of Asika in evidence, he should proceed to do so. But discussing these would-be witnesses *in vacuo* is improper and inadmissible, I would submit!'

The Elder on the fifth throne asked Counsel for Damnation to explain why he was invoking the names of Mboya and Asika without calling them for evidence.

Apolo-Gyamfi answered, 'I have been advised by Brother Solomon, the Programme Officer for Grand Trials, that the assassination of Tom Mboya might itself become a subject for a major trial in After-Africa. Brother Solomon has therefore advised against inviting Mr Mboya to a trial on a related theme at this juncture.'

The Elder on the fifth throne said, 'In that case, Counsel, you should refrain from discussing his case altogether. The objection lodged by Counsel for Salvation is hereby sustained.'

Whereupon Apolo-Gyamfi begged leave to rest, leaving the platform for the next stage of the proceeedings.

21

Hamisi's voice rang out with a startling announcement. 'I call for George Gordon, the Lord Byron!'

There was a moment of collective stupification, as members of the multitude looked at each other in utter bewilderment. The link between the witness and Nigeria seemed to be obscure, to say the least. There the multitudes were reactivated into speculative whisperings, warming their way up towards the poetic link between an Okigbo and a Byron. And yet even there what was the link? Ezra Pound would have been a more relevant poetic witness for the case than Lord Byron, drawn not only from another continent but also from another century.

Yet, if Counsel for Salvation could unearth a connecting theme between Byron and Biafra, he might be on his way towards making legal meta-history. The clouds parted almost in symbolic admission as the skies thundered out the arrival of a witness from After-Europe.

Byron entered from the North Gate of Salvation. That famous slight limp from his malformed foot acquired a majestic conspicuousness in the walk across the field in the Grand Stadium. He was a little fatter than he had been when at his most handsome in the Herebefore, but his face still had that magnetic wildness which had made him the Don Juan of London, and one of the most romantic figures in the history of English literature. His thin moustache curved outwards. He wore a turban with a striking Mediterranean flourish, one end of it hanging resplendently on his left shoulder. Byron climbed up on to the Stage of Decision, and was then escorted by Hamisi to the Pulpit of Evidence.

'Say, "I swear to tell the truth, the whole truth and nothing but the truth, so help me Fate".'

Byron gave a sardonic smile and said, 'I cannot see how anyone

109

but the Almighty can swear to tell the whole truth. How would anyone else know that it was the whole truth?'

There was a moment of embarrassment as Hamisi fidgeted. He wanted his surprise witness to make an impression on the Elders, favourable to his case. These procedural wrangles from a witness might alienate some of the Elders.

But Byron saved him by saying, 'However, if you insist on such empty formulae, I do swear to tell the truth, the whole truth, and nothing but the truth.'

Hamisi added, 'So help you Fate.'

Back came the sardonic smile. 'Fate? I've just told you that I regard the whole formula as an empty ritualistic exercise.' Another general moment of embarrassment. 'However, here we go again . . . so help me Fate!'

Gradually Hamisi succeeded in getting Byron into a conversational rather than argumentative mood. His life was recapitulated for that multitude of After-Africa. The background of his difficult father, and his neurotic mother, a descendant of James the First of Scotland.

Hamisi played on Byron's shared interests with Okigbo – a love of the Classics. When Byron entered Cambridge at the age of seventeen he had already been initiated into the Greco-Roman heritage. By that time he had inherited the title from his great-uncle, though at birth there were many others between him and the title, and it had seemed unlikely that he would inherit it.

Both Byron and Okigbo were terrified of the masses, and this had had a profound impact on their concept of freedom. Byron had said in *Don Juan*:

> It is not that I adulate the people . . .
> . . . I wish men to be free
> As much from mobs as kings . . .

Okigbo's intellectual distance, his assertion that he wrote poetry for fellow poets rather than for the ordinary man, his distrust of the platform and of public postures – these were traits somewhat different from Byron's, yet there were common links of semi-withdrawal, of semi-defensiveness, in both men.

What had shocked Okigbo into fighting for Biafra? It was not the fear of intolerant governments, or brutal soldiers in Nigeria. It was that uprising of mobs in the North – the cobbler's neighbours turning against him one fine day in popular indignation.

> ... I wish men to be free
> As much from mobs as kings ...

Yet the social conscience in both Byron and Okigbo lay just beneath their uneasy fear of the mob. Byron had exploded into fame with his first speech in the House of Lords when he had made a passionate defence of one of the first acts of sabotage directed against automation – workers had wrecked newly installed machinery because of fear of losing their jobs. English society was aroused from its torpor. Byron was lionized. 'A living embodiment of political poetry,' some called him. He was regarded as a man of great potential, both for literature and for politics. Women loved him – never were spindly legs and a club foot more decisively overlooked by female ardour. Byron's delicate features and sensual face, together with an interesting pallor, made an irresistible impact on many aristocratic ladies in the London society of his time.

And then Hamisi came to the real point behind his calling Byron to stand in the witness-box. Both Byron and Okigbo were poets who had died in their mid-thirties fighting for a people's freedom. If the ultimate charge against Okigbo was the subordination of art to the politics of the moment, a similar charge could surely be levelled against George Gordon, Lord Byron.

'In 1823 you set out to join the Greek insurgents in their war against the Turks. You joined Prince Mavrocordato at Missolonghi and comitted yourself to the cause of the rebels. Why did you do it?'

Silence descended while Byron's answer to Hamisi's question

was awaited. Byron cast his eyes down for a short while, looked up at Hamisi and said, 'Because I owed it to them.'

Hamisi queried, 'Owed what to whom?'

Byron answered: 'I owed the Greeks my participation in their quest for freedom.'

At this point Hamisi interrupted the questioning to call forth from the echoes of the Herebefore the voice of Kwame Nkrumah as he gave the speech which came to be known as 'the Motion of Destiny', a motion on fundamental constitutional reform prior to independence. On the eve of Ghana's liberty, Nkrumah had referred to Aristotle as 'the master'. Hamisi, quoting another African intellectual, went on to suggest that at that mature stage of African nationalism such an acknowledgement of Aristotle by Nkrumah was not a submission but a conquest; not a retreat into subservience but a move to transcend. In those simple terms, and with confidence, an African was claiming his share of the Hellenic heritage of man.

Hamisi then referred to Julius Nyerere's views on democracy, which saw the Greek and African visions not in consecutive terms of derivation, but in terms of parallel evolution. The voice of Julius Nyerere came vibrating from the Herebefore with the words, 'The appropriate setting for this basic, or pure, democracy is a small community. The city states of Ancient Greece, for example, practised it. And in African society, the traditional method of conducting affairs is by free discussion . . . the elders sit under the big tree, and talk until they agree . . .'

And there was Byron in the great Pulpit of Evidence in After-Africa. It had been on April 19th, 1824, that a cry had gone forth in Missolonghi, echoed from hill to hill across the land of Greece – 'Byron is dead' . . . 'Yes, I owed·it to them.'

Hamisi asked: 'But were you not sacrificing your art? Others could fight for Greece, but only Byron could write Byron's poetry.

Byron answered, 'Yes, but what is poetry without vision? And what is vision without a mind released? By dying for Greece I died for a vision. And death itself is a poetic quest for comprehension.' Byron quoted himself with the words:

For the sword outwears the sheath,
And the soul wears out the breast.
And the heart must pause to breathe,
And Love itself have rest.

Hamisi paused once again. It had been a risk calling Byron, whom, of course, he had never met, but now he felt he knew him very closely. Byron could be histrionic and unpredictable. But the heavens had been kind; his surprise witness had served the purpose.

Hamisi turned to Counsel for Damnation and inquired if he wished to question the witness. Apolo-Gyamfi nodded. He rose with deliberation. The audience watched with renewed excitement, for Apolo-Gyamfi's slow movements towards the witness-box had all the purposefulness of a fighter. Byron watched the little Ghanaian with interest. He seemed to sense that a fight was in the offing.

'Lord Byron', Apolo-Gyamfi addressed the witness 'will you at last discuss in an open forum your relationship with Augusta?'

Byron stiffened and his eyes flashed the danger signals of anger about to erupt. A large number of people in the audience drew in their breath when they heard Apolo-Gyamfi's statement. Byron's rage was shared by a significant section of that multitude. Apolo-Gyamfi seemed to be purposefully hitting below the belt. What conceivable relevance had Byron's relations with his half-sister Augusta to the Nigerian Civil War? Was Apolo-Gyamfi taking the easy way out by attempting to discredit the witness through moral innuendoes?

The Elders too seemed a little taken aback by this initial thrust from Counsel for Damnation. Hamisi was trying to collect himself.

Meanwhile Byron and Apolo-Gyamfi looked each other steadily in the eye. Byron was furious, but he seemed to be controlling himself admirably. He also seemed determined not to utter a word in response to this question.

Apolo-Gyamfi took the exchange a little further and said, 'I realize you do not take oaths seriously. But you did swear a little earlier to tell the truth and only the truth, though you were sceptical about your own capacity for telling the whole truth. Lord Byron will you tell the Court about Augusta?'

Hamisi at last jumped from his seat, 'I protest, my Elders! Lord Byron's relations with one of his relatives could have no conceivable bearing on this case.'

The Elder on the fifth throne was tempted to say, 'Objection sustained,' yet he felt instinctively that there must be some kind of method in Apolo-Gyamfi's cheap madness. The Elder on the fifth throne therefore addressed Apolo-Gyamfi with the words, 'Will Counsel for Damnation give the Court a clue as to the relevance of this line of questioning?'

'Yes, Oh Elders of Judgement,' said Apolo-Gyamfi. 'I have two reasons for bringing in the affair of the half-sister in this case. One reason concerns the circumstances which led Lord Byron to fight for Greece. The Court is entitled to know how far love of freedom was the real motive behind the noble Lord's adventure.

'But I have a second purpose my Elders for bringing before this Court the affair of Augusta. This second purpose is the symbolic connection between incest and civil war.'

Indignation among the multitudes was beginning to give way to respectful curiosity. Many were seen leaning further forward, as if it needed any such gesture to hear Apolo-Gyamfi's resonant delivery. Even Byron, though still tense with hostile emotions, was now considering the possibility of answering back. The voice of the central Elder announced, 'Objection overruled!'

Apolo-Gyamfi proceeded, 'Lord Byron, let me refresh your memory. The Court is not interested in how many affairs you had, or how many hearts you broke. Many a woman who chased you in London perhaps deserved an ultimate disappointment. But this Court is interested in your affair with your half-sister Augusta, married to her cousin, Colonel Leigh. You and your sister felt a strong attraction to each other transcending the bonds of kinship.

But you also had a conscience about this incestuous relationship. As you yourself put it:

> *We repent, we abjure, we will break from the chain;*
> *We must part, we must fly – to unite it again.*

The silence was total. The audience watched and listened. The Elders concentrated. Hamisi looked worried. But Byron was still silent.

Apolo-Gyamfi continued to 'refresh my Lord's memory'. While still attracted to the half-sister, Byron nevertheless made an inexplicable decision to get married to Anna Isabella Milbanke in January 1815. Byron was not in love with the woman and the money he stood to gain from the match with this heiress was not considerable. It was a match foredoomed to failure. In December 1815 a daughter was born – and Byron had the audacity to have her named Augusta Ada. A few weeks later Byron's wife returned to her family, accusing Byron of incest with his half-sister, and demanding a separation.

The public outcry was immediate and insistent. Pamphleteers went to work, and the name of Byron was attacked in terms fair and foul. The poet left the shores of his country, denounced society for hypocrisy, and set out for distant lands, never to return.

Apolo-Gyamfi continued, 'I put it to this Court that if Okigbo fought for Biafra because he loved his own people, Byron fought for Greece because he was hostile to his own society. Byron carried the banner of freedom in order to disguise his incestuous licence. He loved a Greece which was dead, and hated the living England of his day. It was he himself who described this fusion between nostalgia for the classics and bitterness for his age in the following words:

> *When a man hath no freedom to fight for at home,*
> *Let him combat for that of his neighbours;*
> *Let him think of the glories of Greece and of Rome,*
> *And get knocked on the head for his labours.*

To do good to Mankind is the chivalrous plan,
  And is always as nobly requited;
Then battle for Freedom wherever you can,
  And, if not shot or hanged, you'll get knighted.

Apolo-Gyamfi turned briefly to look at Hamisi as he was making the point, 'My friend, the honourable Counsel for Salvation, thought he would bring before this Court another poet who died in his thirties fighting for freedom. It has been suggested that just as Byron was repaying a debt to the ancestry of Western democracy, Okigbo was repaying a debt to the womb of his identity. We must be careful not to mistake public rationalizations for the inner springs of real motives.'

Byron stirred; he was at last ready to cross swords. 'In your impudence, honourable Counsel, you nevertheless presume to talk about the ancestry of things. You refer to the ancestry of Western democracy. Yes, I did fight for Greece partly because of that ancestry. But you make no reference to the ancestry of love.'

Apolo-Gyamfi waited in a questioning pose. The Elders listened.

Byron continued: 'Yes, I did love Augusta. By the canons of many societies our love was indeed incestuous. But when you talk about the ancestry of things, remember that the most original of all love was incestuous. It started with Adam and Eve – a moment of intimacy with the curve of one's own rib. It continued with Adam's immediate offspring.'

The audience was stirred into exchanges of admiring comments and amused smiles. Adam and Eve, the first parents, were held in affectionate regard throughout the entire After-World. But it was the kind of respect which was allied to a sense of amusement at a couple in many ways very different from all the couples which followed. The reference to a moment of intimacy with the curvature of one's own rib hit at just the right level of indulgent humour towards one's own parents. As for Adam's descendants within those particular branches of the family-tree of humanity, it was indeed correct that incest was the first basis of human reproduction. The origins of love lay in the bed of blatant incest.

Apolo-Gyamfi came back with the rejoinder that 'The Pharaoh of Ptolemic Egypt and Adam, the first father, might have been permitted certain areas of incestuous relationships. That first man in time and that first Egyptian in rank might have been given special dispensations, but Lord Byron was neither.

Byron countered, 'But Lord Byron is interested in both the ancestry of freedom and the ancestry of love. The distinction between family love and sexual love is clearly post-ancestral!'

Apolo-Gyamfi straightened himself and said, 'It is true that some of the earliest sex was between brother and sister. But some of the earliest murder too was the murder of brother by brother. The first love was incestuous; the first murder was fratricide. Shall we encourage brother to kill brother out of reverence for the ancestry of things?'

Byron stiffened, in anticipation of the next thrust. A portion of the audience also sensed the direction which Apolo-Gyamfi was brilliantly taking the argument.

Counsel said to the witness, 'You wrote a tragedy once, did you not? It was published in 1821. The title was *Cain: A Mystery*.' Byron looked at Apolo-Gyamfi steadily, waiting.

'You, as the author, saw the link between evil and fratricide. But you betrayed a grudging admiration for Cain all the same. You made your Cain a pupil of Lucifer. And Lucifer's teaching intensified the revolt of Cain against the conditions he endured. In a fit of passion at Abel's devotion to Jehovah, your Cain struck his brother and killed him.'

Byron was silent, waiting for the argument to be completed. Apolo-Gyamfi continued, 'But you allowed remorse and punishment to ensue upon fratricide. Like yourself after your incest with Augusta, Cain went out into exile after his fratricide. You personally have never admitted remorse, though you may have been punished by that exile. But your tragedy of *Cain* was a tragedy precisely because the act of fratricide entailed guilt and demanded remorse.

'The Nigerian Civil War is the tragedy of Cain writ large. Both fratricide and incest consist in a defilement of kind by kind. Lord

Byron, you were invited here as witness for salvation. But both in your life as Augusta's lover and in your art as the author of *Cain* yours is a testimony of accusation against those who unleashed the horrors of kindred defilement on the population of Nigeria.'

The audience nearly burst out in applause. It had been a memorable exchange. Was it over?

'One more thing, Lord Byron,' said Apolo-Gyamfi. 'This also has something to do with the ancestry of things. Wasn't your mother descended from James the First of Scotland?'

Byron assented.

'You have never been sure whether you were Scottish or English. Even in your satire *English Bards and Scotch Reviewers* the interaction is unmistakable between these two segments. And wasn't it a James the First who united the thrones of England and Scotland? Was the union between the two a mistake?'

Byron answered by referring to the resurgence of Scottish nationalism, reaching its height almost at the same time as the outbreak of the Civil War in Nigeria.

Apolo-Gyamfi said, 'Precisely. The break-up of the British Empire has released forces of distintegration not only in the former colonies like Nigeria, Kenya, and Uganda, but also in the former imperial power itself. The United Kingdom was sensing the disruptive impact of Scottish and Welsh nationalism, and the renewed militancy of Catholic nationalism in Ireland, at precisely the time that the Ibo were plunging into a disastrous quest for separate identity and the Luo and the Kikuyu were testing each other's strength.

'But just because we permitted an empire to break up is not an adequate reason for permitting our respective countries to follow suit. Imperial disintegration is a good thing. Let us not permit it to become less good by allowing it to lead on to national disintegration. By all means let us pause in our affection – but resume again.

> *For the sword outwears the sheath*
> *And the soul wears out the breast,*

And the heart must pause to breathe,
And Love itself have rest.

Apolo-Gyamfi had brought Byron's verses back to him.
They could be made to serve the cause of national cohesion as
they had been made to serve the cause of rebellious freedom.

Salisha in the hundred-and-seventy-third row in the Grand Stadium looked concerned.

22

The multitudes were reassembling for what could be the last day
of the trial. Discussion of the Byronic exchanges of the previous
day was still going on. What a performance by all the three main
actors in that drama! Hamisi's boldness in inviting Byron and
establishing a shared link between him and Christopher Okigbo;
Byron's own facility of repartee in the course of exchanges; but
above all Apolo-Gyamfi's virtuoso performance.

Even the concluding move he contrived was impressive. After
he had taken Byron ruthlessly through incest and fratricide and
converted him virtually into a witness for damnation, Apolo-
Gyamfi adroitly changed the mood. He made a little speech about
Scottish nationalism in relation to the phenomenon of post-imperial fragmentation, and proceeded to draw Byron into an infor-
mal discussion about the age-old interaction between England and
Scotland. It was a brief exchange, but effectively done. It succeeded in easing Byron's tension and made him feel more a participant in a conversation, than a vanquished foe in a debate.

They even mentioned Scotland's disproportionate leadership in
some intellectual activities in Britain, and compared this with the
disproportionate Ibo leadership in some Nigerian intellectual
ventures. The Scots and the Ibo had more in common than mere
separatist tendencies in a post-imperial mood. Apolo-Gyamfi com-

mented 'Scottish imagination even discovered an important legal principle very dear to us in this After-World, but quite alien to English jurisprudence.'

Hamisi tried to work that one out in the course of the dialogue between Apolo-Gyamfi and Byron, but he was not quite sure which legal principle in the After-World paralleled a similar principle in Scottish law. Apolo-Gyamfi was in any case carrying Byron a little further in this bid to take the tension out of the tail-end of the proceedings.

'Yes, English bards and Scotch reviewers have indeed known moments of passionate interchange. But they have differed without being divided. They have more often been rivals in fellowship.'

Byron agreed. And then, with a brilliantly timed triviality, Apolo-Gyamfi capped the informality with the words, 'I was at that other place, Lord Byron – I read Greats at Christ Church. You are a Cambridge man, Byron, aren't you?'

The visitor smiled and said, 'Yes. I understand you – rivalry in fellowship, differences without division.'

The Court thanked the witness from After-Europe for finding the time to come and facilitate proceedings in a court of law in After-Africa.

But all that had happened yesterday, and was now recalled with some excitement and admiration by many in that assembly of returning listeners. A million murmurs in simultaneous excitement filled the Grand Stadium as the arrival of the Elders was awaited.

At last the skies proclaimed the moment. The nine Elders added the solemnity of their presence to the atmosphere of the Stadium. The two Counsels emerged from their different gates and found their way to the Platform of Decision. It was the turn of Counsel for Damnation to invite a witness, but he had waived his right and granted Hamisi the privilege to call his last witness.

The Elders sat down. Apolo-Gyamfi sat down. Hamisi stood up, waited for the multitude to give him their undivided attention, and then made the startling announcement.

'I call upon Salisha, of the household of Abiranja, to come to the witness-box!'

To those who knew some of the background, Hamisi's choice of his final witness was almost as surprising as his choice of Byron. How could Hamisi take such a risk?

A moment later Salisha appeared from the Salvation Gate. She was a striking woman in her neo-Punjabi dress, with a loose *mtandio* framing her face and falling loosely over her shoulders. She walked somewhat self-consciously across the great field, but with enough composure to give her gait a kind of shy elegance. She had been warned only a few moments before the announcement that Hamisi had chosen to make her the final witness. Her heart sank in despair when this incredible piece of news was communicated to her. Had Hamisi really done his homework on the background of his final witness? Did he know the great risk he was taking in putting her into the witness-stand and exposing her to the probing thoroughness of Apolo-Gyamfi?

The crowd in the Stadium was intrigued. An additional layer of excitement was derived from the simple fact that Salisha was the first female witness in this momentous trial. Hamisi extended his hand to her to help her up the steps on to the Stage of Decision. He then protectively guided her to the *mihrab*.

'Do you swear to speak the truth, the whole truth, and nothing but the truth, so help you Fate?' Hamisi administered the ritual.

There was an unmistakable moment of hesitation, perhaps even of agonizing doubt, before Salisha answered, 'I do.'

Hamisi was perplexed, just as he had been perplexed by the surprise he observed on all sides when he had announced Salisha's name as his culminating witness. With regard to the earlier puzzle, he had concluded that it must be unorthodox to call in a witness from under one's own roof in the After-World. After all both he and Salisha shared Abiranja's protective hospitality. They might be presumed to have discussed certain aspects of the case. And even if the precise nature of the testimony had not been analysed in advance, a witness of such close proximity to Counsel was a choice which deliberately tested the outer limits of propriety. At least this was the theory which Hamisi advanced to himself to explain the degree of extra surprise which his announcement of Salisha's name seemed to have occasioned.

Hamisi then proceeded to ask her a few questions to reveal her background more fully. Yes, she had been born to a relatively distinguished Hausa family, though not among the most distinguished. At the age of eight she went to stay with her aunt in the Eastern Region, whose husband had been a successful general shopkeeper in Enugu. Her aunt was relatively educated in religious terms. She could translate a substantial part of the Qur'an. For a woman she was also well versed in *fiqh*. But she was relatively unorthodox in her views, and had a touch of feminist militancy in her. She felt strongly that women, 'especially Muslim women', should exercise more influence in public affairs. She therefore believed in women's secular as well as religious education.

Salisha's father was the aunt's younger brother. Aunt Maryam had finally managed to persuade her younger brother, Bemedi, to let her have the daughter to be brought up as what her aunt called 'a woman of real consequence'.

At first she was sent to a mixed school in Enugu, but her mother protested when she heard about it. The girl was then transferred to a girls' school not far from Enugu, and rapidly established herself as among the most promising. Salisha's name at that time was Aisha.

She went up north to Zaria to visit her parents quite often, but her real home now was with her aunt Maryam and the aunt's husband, Ahmadu.

Later on, a special tutor was engaged to give Aisha extra lessons at home. A sense of rivalry with the Ibo neighbours in Enugu might have been a contributory factor towards the extra attention that Aisha's education received from her aunt and uncle. But whatever the reasons, it paid dividends. Aisha got a First Grade in the Cambridge School Certificate, and later amply satisfied the entry requirements into Ibadan University. She was among the very first girls to be admitted into Ibadan, and certainly the first and only Northern girl during her entire period at Ibadan.

She got a good Upper Second class degree in English, and this created quite a sensation in the North as a whole. There were some who disapproved of this level of female education, certainly in institutions like Ibadan which were basically male institutions, and almost entirely non-Muslim as well. But even among the critics there was a creeping sense of pride that one of their girls had managed to shine in a Southern institution, and had in fact done better than any other woman in any subject in that year at Ibadan.

Aisha got a scholarship with ease to go to Leeds University in England for her Master's degree. Her thesis at Leeds was on Alexander Pope as a satirist.

Hamisi asked here, 'Did you know about Okigbo's poetry when you were at Leeds?'

Salisha answered, 'No, not then. When I left Leeds I went home for a while, both to Zaria and to Enugu, and began to sense the literary revival which was taking place in our midst. But it was not until two years later that I received a copy of *Heavensgate* to review for a broadcasting programme. My review was broadcast in all the three Regions of Nigeria. Until then I had been doing some freelance journalism, writing articles on different cultural subjects. Several West African newspapers bought my stuff, and I had two articles published in London, one in the *New Statesman* and one in *The Observer*. But it was my review of Okigbo's poetry which firmly decided my area of specialization. From then on, I began to see myself as primarily a professional critic of literature. I hoped to write books of literary criticism, as well as do broadcasts.'

The questioning was getting a little warmer, perhaps too warm for the comfort of the questioner and his witness. But inevitably the discussion took the Court to London, and the few months' assignment that Salisha (then Aisha) was given by the Transcription Centre to prepare a series of programmes on the literary renaissance in Africa – fiction, poetry, and drama. The Transcription Centre in London specialized in selling these programmes at reasonable rates to African broadcasting stations. The venture itself was a useful contribution towards the diversification of African radio programmes at an acute moment of need. The Transcription Centre tapped mainly African talent available in England among students and a few African settlers in Britain. But occasionally the Centre actually commissioned a major undertaking by a leading African artist or critic. Miss Aisha Bemedi had been commissioned to do such a major assignment when the B.B.C. in London heard of her presence and invited her to the studios at Bush House to discuss the latest collection of Christopher Okigbo's poetry with the B.B.C. moderator, Hamisi Salim.

At this point Salisha cast her eyes down, and Hamisi proceeded to divert the discussion more firmly towards analysing the meaning of Christopher Okigbo.

'Yes,' said Salisha, 'many of us accepted Okigbo as a fellow Nigerian and were proud of him. Sometimes the brilliance of a few individuals serves as a social cement. Nationalism is nothing if it is not a capacity to have shared heroes. We were proud as Nigerians because we seemed to be in the lead in several spheres of cultural endeavour. We seemed to have the best novelist in the English language, the best playwright in the English language, and a galaxy of the best poets.'

Salisha went on to suggest that the idea of a nation could sometimes be a little too abstract, and hence a little too cold, to command ready human allegiance. To give the idea of Nigeria warmth, it was often necessary either to personify it metaphorically, or more effectively to give it specific human form in national heroes. That was one reason why in the Herebefore ancestor-worship was so important, not only among tribes but also within nations. Ancestor-worship was to a considerable degree a case of hero-worship.

'But Nigeria was a newly invented nation. To a certain extent we needed to invent national heroes as well. While Ghanaians under Nkrumah concentrated all their hero-worship on the Osagyefo, we in Nigeria decided to have multiple idols. Our new authors and poets were among those idols.'

Hamisi asked, 'But was Okigbo interested in the concept of Nigeria? Were you as Nigerians worshipping an idol who was indifferent to your fortunes?'

It was here that Salisha mentioned Okigbo's attachment to a Northern woman. Hamisi, with a twinkle in his eye, interrupted to ask: 'In other words, Miss Bemedi, Christopher Okigbo – like the cobbler Vincent who gave evidence here earlier – was an Ibo who had known the conquering power of Northern womanhood?'

Salisha smiled and cast her eyes down in embarrassment. Much of the audience also smiled in gallant amusement.

Salisha continued the story with an elaboration of Okigbo's inner commitment to the concept of one Nigeria, disguised behind a façade of proud isolationism. She had met him on two occasions, and was quite satisfied that until 1966 Okigbo's own disenchantment with events in Nigeria was the disenchantment of a Nigerian rather than an Ibo. But the Northern massacres of May and September 1966 had been profoundly disturbing to many an Ibo intellectual.

'To get back to the fundamental question, was Okigbo's commitment to the Ibo cause following the massacres a betrayal of his art?' Hamisi inquired.

Salisha admitted that his literary output suffered as a result of the military engagement. But she hastened to emphasize that Okigbo's intention had been to combine patriotism with poetry. As soon as he arrived in Biafra following the exodus of the Ibo from the rest of Nigeria, Okigbo joined Chinua Achebe in forming and running a publishing company called Citadel Books Limited, with offices at 14 Station Road, Enugu. Salisha referred to Okigbo's letter in the publication *Cultural Events* in May 1967 in which he outlined the publishing plans of the company. Part of the commitment of this company was to education – the production of books for primary, secondary, and university needs. Okigbo had said, 'Naturally our emphasis in this our first year of operation will be on primary school books specifically written for Eastern Nigerian children.'

But he also asserted that from 1967 they would, in addition, be engaged in producing works of more substantial literary significance. And then, as if willed by Salisha's narrative impetus, the prose words of Christopher Okigbo once again echoed in the Grand Stadium.

We publish four titles in the series, Citadel African poets: my own 'Elegies of Thunder', Gabriel Okara's 'Poems', George Awoonor-Williams' 'Messages', and Emmanuel Obiechina's 'Understanding Modern African Poetry'. These together with two periodical publications, 'Mbari' (a monthly magazine of the arts), and 'African Writing' (an annual anthology), should represent our own modest contribution to the survival of Africa.

When the Civil War broke out on July 6, 1967, Okigbo joined the Biafran army as a major, leaving Achebe to administer the publishing company.

'Had Okigbo by then decided to turn his back on literature and concentrate on war?' Hamisi asked.

Salisha answered that Okigbo had in fact returned from the war front to Enugu to have long-term discussions with Achebe on the work of the company. He continued to retain a close interest in the future of literature.

He was involved with a group, of which Achebe was also a member, which had plans to launch a magazine called *New Society*, designed to provide a forum for analysing political and moral issues, in relation to cultural imperatives in the new society of Biafra.

Then came September 1967. It was a year since the worst massacres of Northern Nigeria. A lot had happened since then, including the spilling of more Nigerian blood. As that month of September '67 came to a close, two events of some literary importance took place. The house of Africa's leading novelist in the English language, Chinua Achebe, was bombed in Enugu. But the artist lived to tell the tale. Five days later one of Africa's most gifted poets, Christopher Okigbo, was killed on the war front at Nsukka.

Also in ruins amongst all that debris of destruction and mutilation was one small idea symbolic of Okigbo's resilient interest in literature – the idea of 'Citadel Books Limited'.

Hamisi was satisfied with the testimony. 'Thank you, Miss Bemedi.'

He then turned to Apolo-Gyamfi and said, 'Your witness, Counsel.'

What Hamisi did not notice was the sense of apprehension, almost of dread, which had returned to Salisha's eyes as Apolo-Gyamfi rose to cross-examine.

23

Apolo-Gyamfi stood for a moment or two by the witness-box partly for effect, but also because he wanted to be sure about the propriety of what he was about to do. Many in the audience held their breath, sensing a moment of great delicacy.

Then Apolo-Gyamfi started: 'That Christopher Okigbo had not intended to turn his back on art as he marched towards war may indeed have been a mitigating factor. He hoped to combine the skills of the battlefield with the skills of the pen, the sound of cannon-fire with the promptings of the muse, an undertaking to kill with a commitment to create. It is up to the Court to decide whether this tragic ambivalence was tenable from the start. What we do know is that Okigbo's intentions came to nought. The literary and publishing ambitions perished as two more casualties in all that scheming for vengeance. In reality, if not by intention, Christopher Okigbo did turn his back on art as he marched to the battlefield.'

Apolo-Gyamfi saw Hamisi shaking his head in irritation. He grabbed the opportunity and said, 'As Counsel for Salvation seems particularly disturbed by what I have just said, would the Court be indulgent enough to permit him to correct my error before I go on?'

As the Elder on the fifth throne nodded, Hamisi, who had not intended to say anything, took advantage of the offer to make this comment: 'You seem to make no distinction between a defensive war and a war of aggression. Okigbo did not take to the battlefield for reasons of vengeance, as honourable Counsel seems to suggest.'

The dread in Salisha's eyes deepened. The eyes of Apolo-Gyamfi brightened militantly.

Apolo-Gyamfi said, 'I'm less sure than my honourable friend about where military action ceases to be aggressive and becomes defensive. Who shares the guilt of the Nigerian Civil War? Are you sure it lies so exclusively in the hearts of rioting peasants in the villages of the North?'

Hamisi was going to answer, but then decided he should not strain the indulgence he had been granted too far.

Apolo-Gyamfi continued: 'Witness for Salvation brought before you earlier in these proceedings that unfortunate cobbler from Kano, Vincent Obika. The riots in September 1966 were reported to have been ignited by a broadcast from a foreign radio station reporting that Hausa were being killed and mutilated in the Eastern Region. Counsel for Salvation, apparently with little prior research, presumed to declare to this distinguished Court that there was not a shred of evidence behind that report.'

A sense of great solemnity had now entered Apolo-Gyamfi's voice. A number of people in the audience held their breath. Salisha was biting her lip nervously. Abiranja on the two-hundred-and-seventh row of the Grand Stadium looked deeply concerned.

Apolo-Gyamfi said, 'I hate the opportunity that Counsel for Salvation has given me. But it is my duty to conduct my side of the case with as much vigour and as much thoroughness as circumstances permit. Counsel for Damnation did not know of any evidence of disturbances in the East prior to the rioting in the North. Yet Counsel for Salvation has himself brought to the witness-box here and now a tragic piece of evidence.'

Hamisi looked up sharply, uncertain of what it all meant. Salisha's eyes were full of unshed tears.

The Elder on the fifth throne nodded to Apolo-Gyamfi encouraging him to go through with the cross-examination, regardless of the delicate nuances.

Apolo-Gyamfi turned to the witness and said, 'I am very sorry, Miss Bemedi. But we have to force you to recall it all.'

Yes, she had been in Enugu two days *before* the Northern riots of September 1966. She never found out for certain how it all started, but her uncle came home in great agitation. They had set his shop on fire. There were conflicting stories as to how the rioting in Enugu started. Rumours had it that it started with a political argument between a Hausa man and an Ibo. But there were other rumours, including the rumour that a Hausa taxi driver had knocked down an Ibo boy and killed him. Perhaps it did not matter how it started. Perhaps the situation was all set in tinder readiness for the stray match to set it aflame.

'Then they came to Uncle Ahmadu's house, led there by none other than Obi. Obi was a debtor to my uncle, a beneficiary of the more lenient side of my uncle's nature, and yet also a rival in the tie-dye textile trade. He brought a gang of fellow Ibo, eager to settle old scores with poor Ahmadu. They were armed with sticks and, in two cases, with knives.'

Salisha went on to narrate how her uncle went out to try and reason with the aggressive visitors. They insulted him as a 'Hausa blood-sucker' and made some disparaging remarks about his religion. There was a good deal of shouting. 'But there was one piece of abuse which strained even my uncle's patience to breaking-point. They shouted that it was time that the East was rid of "Mohammedan filth".'

Almost instinctively Ahmadu's arm rose and he swiped at the jeering face responsible for that taunt. 'They then descended upon him, indifferent to his old age, and with pitiless ferocity!'

Ahmadu's wife dashed out of the door, screaming, and waving a ridiculous broom. 'Aunt Maryam was so angry with them.' But they did not spare her either. It was then that Aisha Bemedi made a move. She dragged herself out, stood leaning on the door at the threshold, shouting 'Stop it! Stop it!' She turned to some of the spectators around, urging passionately, 'Stop them, for God's sake, stop them!'

But instead of stopping the brutality against the elderly couple, two men stepped forward, caught hold of Aisha's arms, pinned them behind her back, turned her round, and forced her back into the house. Aisha was at first absolutely flabbergasted, and then totally enraged. For a minute she thought that because she was pregnant they were turning her back so that she would not see that pitiless brutalizing of her foster parents. It was when the two men pushed her into her aunt's bedroom that she was startled into the horrifying realization of what they were about to do.

She struggled, and wrenched to pull her right arm free, and started scratching the face of one of the men. She immediately felt a sharp pain on the chin, as she stumbled backwards and banged her head against the dressing-table. They hit her again and again. And when she lay exhausted on the floor, they started to strip her. She was a little dazed, and her nose and mouth were bleeding. She felt very sick.

A third man entered the room. He saw what his two comrades were about to do, and took the initiative in facilitating the operation. He pulled down two pillows from the bed, and shoved them underneath Aisha's buttocks. Her condition made rape an uncomfortable posture even for the violator – unless the expansion of her thighs was facilitated by the support of raised pillows underneath. They raped her, perhaps half a dozen of them, perhaps ten of them or more. Half-way through two policemen came. Aisha, in hazy consciousness, thought the ordeal was over and she was about to be rescued. But the two policemen took their turn in the queue, saying, 'Let us taste the Hausa bitch!'

Aisha began to bleed between her thighs, but it did not seem to put them off. Her head was thumping hard, and the term 'Hausa bitch! Hausa bitch!' kept hammering away in her consciousness, almost rhythmically with the tempo of her latest violator in action.

The shadows started closing in. Her physical agony began to diminish; the man on top of her seemed to melt; the rest of the bystanders in that room were receding beyond the infinite.

'You never recovered consciousness,' Apolo-Gyamfi said kindly to the strong woman in the witness-box, tears of pain pouring down her cheeks, yet still resolute enough to confront the questions from Counsel for Damnation. Hamisi's cheeks were also wet, as he listened in agony to this horror.

Apolo-Gyamfi continued, 'And you lost the baby?'

She turned to look at Hamisi, and a look of anguish passed between them. Salisha's voice broke as she said, 'The baby was due in another two weeks. That long queue of barbarians killed it, as they killed me!' She was still looking at Hamisi, a look of shared bereavement.

Hamisi rose slowly, groaning from the depths of his being, and saying hoarsely, 'No! No!'

Salisha said, 'Yes, darling, yes!' as she broke down completely and sobbed the sobs of total anguish.

Apart from her sobs and Hamisi's groans there was a silence in the Grand Stadium, half pitying, half embarrassed. The solemn figure of Abiranja was then seen walking across the lawn, his white *kanzu* shimmering in the majesty of movement. The multitudes looked on, as Abiranja climbed the steps of the Stage of Decision. He knelt before the Elders, without saying a word. The Elder on the fifth throne nodded his head, Abiranja rose and went to the witness-pulpit. Salisha was still sobbing. Abiranja climbed the *mihrab*, put his long reassuring arm round her shoulders and guided her down the *mihrab*, away from the Stage of Decision, and onwards across the lawn. As they walked down, the Grand Stadium was filled once again with lines from Okigbo.

> *For the far* removed there is wailing:

> *For the far removed;*
> *For the Distant . . .*

> The wailing is for the fields of crop:

The drums' lament is:
They grow not . . .

The wailing is for the fields of men:

For the barren wedded ones;
For perishing children . . .

The wailing is for the Great River:

Her pot-bellied watchers
Despoil her . . .

Salisha had stopped sobbing. She walked away, guided by Ab-iranja, beyond the vision of onlookers. Hamisi had stopped groaning and was sitting there dazed and unsure.

He remembered that night in London. He remembered the strategy from the B.B.C. studios, to the restaurant for dinner, to his own flat and the literary discussion. He remembered the music. He remembered his conquest at last, with Aisha in his arms.

He remembered waking up the next morning and finding himself alone in bed. He remembered all those days of trying to re-establish contact, of checking up with the Student Adviser of the Nigeria Office, of writing letters care of the Transcription Centre. He remembered Aisha's total exit from his life.

As he sat there in the Grand Stadium not all the segments of the great puzzle had come into place yet, but they were to do so before long. All he knew for the time being was that he had made Aisha Bemedi pregnant that fateful evening in London. He was to know later of the pain of her discovery, of the terrible indecision as to whether she should have an abortion or not. She could not stay in London much longer; she didn't know how to face a number of friends. She could not go to Zaria with the shame of a child acquired in distant lands from a total stranger. All the worst predictions of orthodox Muslim neighbours who had disapproved of her education and her exposure to the Western world would now be horribly vindicated.

There was of course only one place to run back to. That was to Aunt Maryam in Enugu.

Aunt Maryam had been visibly disturbed when she had first confessed her condition. Aisha had cried bitterly on her aunt's shoulder. The elderly woman, after a moment of hesitation, put her arm reassuringly round her niece and stroked the girl's hair with her other hand. In a sense Aunt Maryam felt she herself might be to blame. Her feminist militancy had managed to produce a highly modern and cultured young Hausa woman, the first female Master of Arts of her community. But she had also exposed her niece to other dangers. Now she had to support her in her moment of torment, and see her through.

But then that ugly day came. Ahmadu was killed outside his own home. Aisha was raped to death, and perished with her child. Aunt Maryam survived, but she was never the same again. Her brother, Bemedi, came to fetch her to take her back to Zaria. They cried in each other's arms over the fate of Ahmadu and Aisha. They returned sadly back to their own segment of Nigeria.

Hamisi, Counsel for Salvation, sat there in the Grand Stadium, dazed and empty.

24

The previous session had been exhausting for many members of the audience. In the history of Grand Trials, there had been few scenes of such tragic embarrassment. Counsel for Salvation had made a massive miscalculation. It was quite clear regarding Salisha's background that he had not gone to the Bureau of Information prior to summoning her before the Court. If he had gone to the Bureau of Information, as he had done when briefing himself about Lord Byron, he would have had at least a brief account of how Aisha Bemedi died. This would have been enough of a warning signal against inviting her to the witness-box.

Why had he not gone to the Bureau of Information beforehand?

As it happened, it was because he couldn't bring himself to consult a library book or library cards for details about her life. To him it was like spying on her. The full story of her life had to come from Salisha herself and not from documents and files tucked away in library stacks. And yet, the rules of trial in After-Africa precluded consultation between a prospective witness and the Counsel concerned. Hamisi could not go and ask Salisha to brief him about herself prior to the confrontation in the witness-box.

Why therefore did he call her at all? Partly because it had never occurred to him that there was a major risk. He knew from that memorable discussion in London on the fateful night that, although a Hausa woman, she was deeply drawn towards Okigbo's poetry. A Northern fan of Christopher Okigbo was a tempting witness for salvation in that Grand Trial. Hamisi was so sure he would serve the cause of Okigbo well if, in front of the Court, there came the testimony of a sophisticated Hausa woman in defence of Okigbo's meaning for Nigeria. Hamisi nearly pulled it off, but he acted in ignorance of the circumstances by which Aisha Bemedi stumbled into After-Africa.

Many in the audience spared a moment of pity for Hamisi, as well as for Salisha and her background. The old-timers in the Grand Stadium knew, of course, why it was that the woman bore a different name in After-Africa from that which she had borne in the Herebefore. It was the way in which she died. The grand ambiguity between birth and death – a mother dying because a child was struggling to be born. This by itself would have meant a change of name for the mother. The Assembly of the Ages had decreed a long time ago that demise by ambiguity negated the previous name. After all, such a capitulation was a blurring of the essence of things – a struggle to give life culminating in exhausted death.

But the end of Aisha Bemedi had an additional dimension of ambiguity. It lay in the abuse of the sexual act. She was killed by cumulative rape. Nature's grand design of creativity had been employed as a squalid device of destruction. Again here was a blurring of the essence of things. The new name could echo the old one – but it could not be the same one. Aisha became Salisha.

A lot of speculation went on in the Grand Stadium as to the implications of all the testimony which had emerged in the course of the proceedings. What were the Elders going to decide? They had excused themselves for deliberation and meditation. They were being awaited for the final verdict and judgement.

At last the skies gave way in their thunderous pronouncement. The moment had come. The nine Judges emerged on to the great field, resplendent with all the solemnity of the moment of culmination.

They ascended the Stage of Decision. They ascended their thrones, and nodded permission for the millions to resume their seats. The skies exploded again, and the voice of the Elder on the fifth throne started the long statement of judgement. His voice had the slight hoarseness of age, but there was firmness about it all the same, and full clarity. Men and women, drawn from all the centuries of Africa's human existence, sat there in close attention as the considered wisdom of the Elders revealed itself on this particular issue. The Elder on the fifth throne first explained what it was that had influenced the Council of Grand Trials to decide on making a special case of Christopher Okigbo and the Nigerian Civil War.

'It occurred to us that this whole tragedy was once again the Curse of the Trinity unfolding itself in the drama of Africa's existence. Let us remind ourselves, Oh fellow citizens of After-Africa, of the meaning of the Curse of the Trinity in relation to this old continent of ours.'

The Christian story of three in one, and one in three, had in part been a prophecy about Africa, and in part a post-mortem on Africa.

At the structural level there was the trinity as the basis of Africa's geography, the Tropic of Capricorn, the Equator, the Tropic of Cancer. Of all the continents of the world only Africa is central enough to be traversed by all three basic latitudes. The Equator almost cuts the African continent into two halves – such is the centrality of Africa to the global scheme of things.

135

The grand triangle of the oceans is also part of the Curse of the Trinity in Africa's geography. The Mediterranean to the north, the Atlantic Ocean to the west, and the Indian Ocean to the east. The Red Sea pointed an accusing finger at a continent northwards which later extended its guilty hegemony over the fortunes of Africa.

The Curse of the Trinity followed Africa's historical course. The triangle of the Asiento – beads from Europe to West Africa, slaves from West Africa to the Americas, sugar from the Americas to Europe.

The Curse of the Trinity bedevilled African culture. On this, one son of Africa, Kwame Nkrumah, had put his finger on the tripartite destiny. At this moment the Elders willed testimony from the Herebefore by Kwame Nkrumah, and a voice responded filling the cosmos with the following reflections from that controversial son of the continent:

African society has one segment which comprises our traditional way of life; it has a second segment which is filled by the presence of the Islamic tradition in Africa; it has a final segment which represents the infiltration of the Christian tradition and culture of western Europe into Africa, using colonialism and neo-colonialism as its primary vehicles. These different segments are animated by competing ideologies. But since society implies a certain dynamic unity, there needs to emerge an ideology which, genuinely catering for the needs of all, will take the place of the competing ideologies, and so reflect the dynamic unity of society, and be the guide to society's continual progress.

The Grand Stadium listened to his voice from the Herebefore. It did have elements in it that were clearly derived from the rhetorical fibre of the old Osagyefo, but there were other strands in that voice as it continued.

With true independence regained, however, a new harmony

136

needs to be forged, a harmony that will allow the combined presence of traditional Africa, Islamic Africa, and Euro-Christian Africa, so that this presence is in tune with the original humanist principles underlying African society. Our society is not the old society, but a new society enlarged by Islamic and Euro-Christian influences. A new emergent ideology is therefore required, an ideology which can solidify in a philosophical statement, but at the same time an ideology which will not abandon the original humanist principles of Africa.

The Elders permitted the voice from the Herebefore to proclaim Nkrumah's own solution to the Curse of the Trinity in relation to Africa's cultural personality.

Practice without thought is blind; thought without practice is empty. The three segments of African society ... coexist uneasily; the principles animating them are often in conflict with one another ... What is to be done then? I have stressed that the two other segments, in order to be rightly seen, must be accommodated only as experiences of the traditional African society. If we fail to do this our society will be racked by the most malignant schizophrenia.

The voice of Nkrumah from the Herebefore completed its testimony. It had touched on a prophecy of doom. It had touched on the Curse of the Trinity.

Nkrumah himself had been known to prescribe solutions to the problems. *Consciencism* was his solution to the tripartite cultural personality which had afflicted Africa, but he also had the solution of an all-African union. The Elders at this juncture permitted another voice from the Herebefore – it was from an African political scientist seeking to understand the Curse of the Trinity as it affected *Pax Africana* in the first few years of Nkrumah's leadership of post-independent Africa. The voice from the clouds argued thus:

In practice, it was into three major categories that Africa could be divided. The categories were Arab Africa, English-speaking Negro Africa, and French-speaking Negro Africa. Nkrumah began by trying to establish closer ties with each ... but in the years which followed, Nkrumah's role in bringing together the different segments of Africa varied according to segment. In relations between Arab Africa and Negro Africa Nkrumah was, on the whole, a unifying factor. But in relations between English-speaking Negro Africa and French-speaking Negro Africa Nkrumah was, on balance, a divisive factor.

The voice of the political scientist receded into oblivion. The Elder on the fifth throne continued the story of the Curse of the Trinity on Africa's fortunes.

It was not just a trinity of major inter-territorial languages. There was also a trinity of areas of racial domination. Above the Tropic of Cancer was the Africa of the Arabs. Around the Tropic of Capricorn was the Africa in Caucasian control. Between Cancer and Capricorn traversing the Equator lay much of the Africa of Black destiny.

And the young states of this intermediate sector had emerged into independence and sought a basis of organization. The Curse of the Trinity reared its head. The world was to consist of the West, the East, and the non-aligned. In the ethos of the non-aligned the Curse of the Trinity transformed itself into a sin of ambiguity.

And then a third voice from the Herebefore filled the cosmos. It was the voice of Leopold Senghor. His testimony was brief.

For my part, I think Afro-Asianism has been superceded, for this form of solidarity should be extended to Latin America and to the Third World in general.

The Curse of the Trinity had now been extended to the concept of development and the division of the world by the yardstick of that development. There was a world of the developed East, there was another world of the developed West, and there was a *third world* of the underdeveloped.

But in that third world of the underdeveloped there was a trinity within a trinity. For the Third World was *tricontinental*. They had even formed a tricontinental organization, consisting of Africa, Asia, and Latin America. Africa was the most underdeveloped of those three continents. The Curse of the Trinity determined Africa's rank – just as it had done centuries earlier when Africa was the weakest of the three known continents of the Ancient World. That was five thousand years and more before Columbus discovered the outer horizon of the setting sun. History was yet to record even the bare notion of Terra Australis Incognita. The snowy mists of Antarctica had yet to reveal their continental secrets. Prior to all these, and much else besides, there was a Europe, there was an Asia, and there was an Africa, in minimal communion with each other. They had yet to bear those names, but the Curse of the Trinity had already sentenced them to everlasting contact.

Here the Elder on the fifth throne paused for a minute to let this momentous account of the Curse of the Trinity in Africa's destiny consolidate itself in the minds of the audience as the grand context of the Okigbo trial. And yet, what did it all have to do with Okigbo and the Nigerian Civil War? The audience listened, deeply moved, sensing the nearness of comprehension, and yet for the time being, in a state of baffled paralysis. The Elder on the fifth throne continued the narration.

'Yes, indeed, Nigeria eventually came into being. Islam, Euro-Christianity, and indigenous tradition struggled to forge a new personality in a single nation. Nigeria was Africa in embryo. But superimposed over this eternal tripartite tension was the mundane accident of three regions in a Federal Nigeria, each dominated by one of three major tribes. The Curse of the Trinity was chasing Africa to the very embryo of its Nigerian manifestation.'

The Elders of After-Africa had watched the events which culminated in the Nigerian Civil War. After long meditation, it was decided to take judicial account of this latest painful infliction of the Curse upon the continent.

'The Elders chose to put on trial a poet, partly because of the poet's role in that great drama linking the living, the dead, and those yet to be born – again a trinity of divine organization, sometimes understood at its most painful in African traditional religions. But even a modern poet, by the very nature of what goes on within him, provides a fitting subject for examination where the Curse of the Trinity has hit again.'

Almost in response to these words Okigbo's poetry briefly punctuated the Elder's narration.

> *Scar of the crucifix,*
> *over the breast,*
> *by red blade inflicted*
> *by red-hot blade,*
> *on right breast witnesseth . . .*

> Messiah will come again
> After the argument in heaven
> Messiah will come again . . .

The Elder on the fifth throne paused again letting both his narration and the poetic interruption settle into the atmosphere of the Grand Stadium.

The Elder then referred to the old Judaic misunderstanding about the principle of analogy in divine judgement. The concept of 'an eye for an eye, a tooth for a tooth' was never intended to be a principle of exact retribution; it was intended to be a principle of analogy as a guide to balance.

'The principle of analogy in divine judgement had to be invoked in this case also. We were putting an aspect of the Curse of the Trinity on trial. The approach to such a trial had itself to have a trinial foundation. The Counsel for Salvation, the Counsel for Damnation, and the accused Christopher Okigbo, were all on trial for different things. A tripartite case to deal with a tripartite curse.

140

We were trying the Counsel for Salvation for the sin of miscalculation. There was the miscalculation on the highroad between Voi and Nairobi; and the miscalculation in a moment of pleasure one night in London. We were trying Counsel for Damnation for the sin of impatience on that foolish night at Oxford. We were trying Christopher Okigbo for Nigeria and its agony, in relation to that primordial curse in Africa's fortunes.'

The Elder pointed out that in the case of Hamisi the sin of miscalculation was sometimes connected with the sin of inadequate concentration. Adequate concentration on the implications of certain situations could have averted some of the consequences arising through these incautious tendencies.

Before the actual trial opened in After-Africa, Hamisi was briefly subjected to a test of concentration pure and simple. It was when he went to the Refresher Room in the Grand Stadium to consult with Jacob Alobi. As a Muslim, Hamisi had been prepared from childhood for the sensuous side of After-Africa. Of all the great religions, Islam was the most frank in its image of the ultimate pleasures of the human personality. The rivers of wine and milk in the Hereafter, the promise of *houries*, those female companions for the faithful after death – these were promises which anticipated Freud's interpretation of the springs of human motivation by a thousand years.

Yet Hamisi, brought up from the age of nine to know about the women who awaited the faithful beyond the grave, nevertheless staggered back in embarrassment as he saw those two football teams naked in the Refresher Room, alternating between the massage and the act of love. Hamisi went there to collect testimony, and Jacob Alobi had provided several intimations of some of the essential elements of Nigeria's background. But surrounding Hamisi was *hourie* sensuality, and there before him was Alobi himself, his manhood erect, massaged by a naked woman. Could this impair Hamisi's powers of concentration as the details poured forth from Alobi's exuberant reflections and reminiscences? And would Hamisi be tempted to take a moment of pleasure although

141

he had only a week in which to prepare a brief on behalf of Christopher Okigbo?

Hamisi had passed the test of concentration in the Refresher Room. What remained was the sin of miscalculation to be expiated in the trial itself.

In relation to this sin, Hamisi had failed. Byron's testimony was adroitly converted by Apolo-Gyamfi to serve the purposes of damnation, but the invitation to Lord Byron was not necessarily an instance of miscalculation on Hamisi's part. He was simply outwitted by Apolo-Gyamfi. But the invitation to Salisha Bemedi was a monumental act of miscalculation. His motives in not consulting the Bureau of Information might have been honourable, but in that case he should not have chosen a witness about whom he did not have full knowledge. It was that same streak of miscalculation which had thrown him out of his car, somersaulting his way to death near Voi; the same streak of carelessness which before that had plunged a night's intimacy into a tragedy of shame and the anguish of ambiguous death at the end of it; that same, or miscalculation, which had made Hamisi drag that woman once again into a situation where she had to relive in agonized and glaring exposure her humiliating final hour in the Herebefore.

Apolo-Gyamfi, on the other hand, had expiated his old sin of impatience. He had sat through the testimony of important witnesses, listening to arguments of potential harm to his side. He had declined to cross-examine Vincent Obika after his agony of relived terror – a piece of good judgement and of good taste. He had awaited his turn with Byron, and drawn him out effectively. He had had the patience to waive the tempting idea of an additional witness of his own – preferring instead to see what he could do in the cross-examination with witnesses chosen by his opponent. Apolo-Gyamfi was acquitted by the Elders. He was now to take his great bath of initiation, in the Holy Well of Zam-Zam. That was in fact the well from whose womb the River Ganges was born back on earth in another continent.

As for the case of Christopher Okigbo, an important principle of After-African jurisprudence had now to be invoked. It was a principle echoed by Scottish law on earth. True, Okigbo had in an important sense turned his back on art and taken to war. But there were enormous mitigating circumstances. The pull of common humanity was not to be despised; nor the compulsion of kinship laughed at. In any case, Counsel for Damnation had not succeeded in making too sharp a distinction between art and nationhood.

Again the Elder's narration was punctuated by a voice in cosmic testimony. It was the voice of Oscar Wilde.

Every single work of art is the fulfilment of a prophecy. For every work of art is the conversion of an idea into an image. Every single human being should be the fulfilment of a prophecy. For every human being should be the realization of some ideal, either in the mind of God or in the mind of man.

The Elder on the fifth throne added, 'What Oscar Wilde might also have mentioned is that every nation in the making is a potential work of art. For the nation too is often the conversion of an idea into an image. The Nigerian nation was in the process of being converted slowly, painfully, from an idea into an image. Okigbo was momentarily distracted from this image, though not in total innocence. As his poetry would tell us:

> *The Sunbird sings again*
> *From the* LIMITS *of the dream . . .*
> *Her image distracts*
> *With the cruelty of the rose . . .*

'The verdict in the case of Christopher Okigbo, must, for the time being, remain *Not Proven*.'

That vast multitude, drawn from every part of the continent, from every age of the history of Africa, saw the two levels of judgement. One level was concerned with the personalities themselves – Hamisi, Apolo-Gyamfi, and Christopher Okigbo. But the

143

principle of analogy in divine jurisprudence was also concerned with the other level of these judgements. These were the verdicts not on the individual persons who had been on trial, but on the roles they had been playing and the values they had personified. The verdict on Counsel for Biafra was *Guilty;* the verdict on Counsel against Biafra was *Not Guilty;* and the verdict on Biafra herself was *Not Proven.*

Those who had championed and defended the cause of Biafra were guilty of a tragic miscalculation. They had exposed those they loved to public anguish. In the full glare of world attention in the Grand Stadium of the Herebefore, they had forced the Ibo to relive the anguish of imminent death which had made them scramble away in terror from more hostile territories. It was a massive miscalculation. More Ibo died in the Nigerian Civil War than could conceivably have died in three decades of rioting in the North.

Those who had opposed the cause of Biafra may, at times, have lacked adequate inner resources of human patience. They might not have always made allowances for the right to be afraid, even if this right did not entail a right to full security. But, on balance, history had turned out to be on the side of those who would not permit the Curse of the Trinity to dismember the embryo of political Africa. Rather than yield to the cunning of the Curse by pulling out the old Eastern Region altogether from tripartite Nigeria, it made better sense to frustrate the Curse by multiplying the Regions of one Nigeria.

As for Biafra herself, the case has to remain *Not Proven.* The Ibo might not have had the right to security in the Africa of their day but they did have the right to be afraid. They, like their champions, had been guilty of miscalculation – and yet did not they have a right to take a gamble? In any case they had suffered – while their supporters cheered them towards disaster from the reassuring safety of a spectator's gallery.

'Was Christopher Okigbo guilty for having tried – and died? The verdict must remain Not Proven! And yet in that very ambiguity lies Okigbo's punishment. He, like all those who fought for

Biafra, must travel through the ages wondering: Was it worth it?'

What of the sentence on Hamisi? The Elders in their wisdom sentenced him to what might be a sad fate of disgrace. Hamisi was sentenced to haunt a lonely baobab tree in Gabon and frighten little children straying near. He was sentenced to reside in that tree at the Elders' pleasure, perhaps for centuries, playing a game of 'scare' on windy evenings and dark nights in the Herebefore. Hamisi's anguish might have been total. The prospect of such a demeaning eternity made him feel stiff and cold.

And then a voice rang out from the audience asking for the Elders' indulgence. Did not the law of After-Africa permit a companion to an immortal the right to seek his permission to accompany another man? Was not the condition simply that the other man had to be someone that the companion had known in the Herebefore? The Elders assented to this interpretation.

'Then I, Salisha Bemedi, formerly known in the Herebefore as Aisha Bemedi, do request the indulgence of the nine Elders of Judgement to let me accompany this accused in disgrace to his new abode in a baobab tree.'

The Court was astonished by the measure of this female sacrifice, particularly after the agonies of that act of miscalculation in the Herebefore.

'My Elders, it was my miscalculation, too.'

Anywhere else that statement might have been a joke. In that context of affirmation of loyalty it was a moving pronouncement. Salisha looked at Abiranja next to her. Abiranja reached out and squeezed her hand and smiled in encouragement. Salisha looked down from those heights of the audience to Hamisi on the Platform of Decision. Hamisi's eyes had tears in them.

And so it is that in a desolate part of Gabon, on a windy evening, children sometimes hear voices reciting poetry to each other. It sounds like a man and a woman.

> . . . Then we must sing, tongue-tied,
> without name or audience,
> Making harmony among the branches.